Yoshiko
and the Gift
of Charms

JULIA SUZUKI

A 'Steve Brookes Publishing' book
www.stevebrookes.com

Illustrations:
Rebecca Ellis

Cover design & layout:
Alex Buxton
maxstardesign@gmail.com

Copy editor:
Bronwyn Robertson
www.theartsva.com

Author:
Julia Suzuki
www.landofdragor.com

First published in 2011 by:
Steve Brookes Publishing, 60 Loxley Road
Stratford-upon-Avon, Warwickshire CV37 7DR
Tel: 01789 267124 / 07801 552538
Email: steve@stevebrookes.com

A CIP catalogue record for this book is available from the British Library
ISBN 978-0-9564145-8-8

Printed and bound in India for Lattitude Press Limited

To the children and the child in us all

Everyone has a special gift and when we discover
it we find that happy place in our hearts

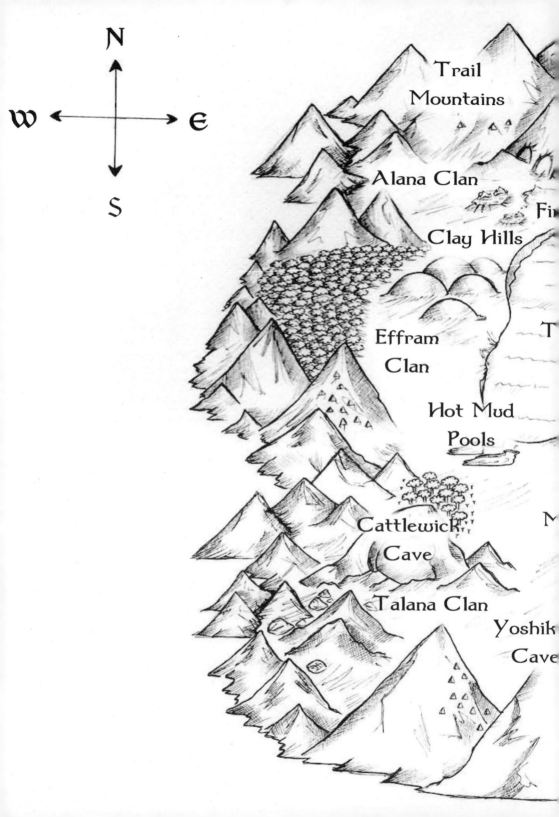

"Romao shuddered, thinking of the legends he had learned in school, where dragons had once been chained as slaves and made to carry heavy loads on their backs."

Chapter One

Romao's Plight

First came the whispers then the rumours. And by the time of New Birth's Eve every dragon seemed to be gossiping that Kiara had laid a strange egg.

Some said it was square, like the toffee-nuts gathered by the sweet-toothed Bushki dragons.

Whilst others claimed they had heard a strange sound from Kiara and Ketu's cave as they had flown overhead, as if the egg were singing.

But the older dragons said it was the sad grey colour of a sickly hatchling, and that when the shell broke the Hudrah would arrive and use the black wicker basket to ferry the infant away.

Since then the cave Kiara shared with Ketu had attracted a constant stream of visitors, eager to find out more about what the egg could mean for the Dragon clans. They were turned away by Ketu and Kiara's Guard Dragon, Romao, who had won the honour of protecting their home during the last stages of the nesting. But now even the loyal young sentry had begun to wonder if there might not be some truth to the whispers and rumours.

Since making her nest Kiara had not moved an inch from her precious egg. Like the other female dragons of Dragor she knew when her time was to lay by the white speckles that appeared on her chest, and had flown out to gather the crystal-rich rocks and chew them into a smooth sand to make her nest. Since settling in her cave to lay the egg she had sat quietly in the same position, gulping up the occasional mouthful of powdery quartz.

Unlike some of the other nesting partners Kiara's mate Ketu was very hard-working. He would have easily afforded Kiara the time to stretch her wings whilst he looked after their nest but since she didn't move from the cave it caused Romao to believe that they were hiding something.

He knew that some of the dragons were worried that a strange egg might mean something terrible for Dragor. Perhaps even discovery by humans.

Romao shuddered, thinking of the legends he had learned in school, where dragons had once been chained as slaves and made to carry heavy loads on their backs. But he chased the feeling away. He truly hoped there was nothing wrong with Kiara's egg.

To keep his mind busy he gazed out into the centre of Dragor to The Fire Which Must Never Go Out.

When Romao had been at Fire School he had asked his teacher why the fire must be kept burning at all times, and the reply had prompted him to make it his life's ambition to be a guard on New Birth's Eve.

"Guarding The Fire of Dragor is the greatest test of discipline and honour that any dragon can have," the teacher had explained, addressing the entire classroom. "A young dragon who qualifies to guard the new hatchlings may one day be granted the right to look after The Fire Which Must Never Go Out. It must burn constantly all day and all night to protect the dragons, as the smoke which rises up keeps us safe from the eyes of humans and our land a secret from those who could be our enemies."

Romao pictured himself, as he had done many times before, as Fire Guard. He was a red-coloured dragon of the Nephan clan, and despite their smaller size Nephans were natural leaders and often won special posts such as fire guarding.

Suddenly Romao heard a little scuffling. He looked down to see a cluster of three young dragons had approached the cave, clearly hoping for a peek at the infamous egg. Dragor had seven different types of dragon, all different colours, and unlike Romao who was a fiery red, the approaching youngsters had bright blue scales and were from the Talana clan.

Nephans were quick and nimble with short narrow wings for agility when turning sharply in the skies. Talanas were large framed with powerful wings, thick skins and a horn which grew out of the centre of their heads. Romao noticed that on these little Talanas their horns had not yet fully grown, and their blue bodies did not yet have the muscular hulk of the older of their kind. But they were already sturdier and with deeper voices than the other small dragons.

The first of the three came forward, snuffling slightly. "We come for news of Kiara's egg," she said in a blunt fashion, sounding amazed at her own daring. "We hear the shell is made of the hardest rock and the hatchling inside will need a horn made of the toughest metal, or it cannot hatch."

Romao sighed. He was tired of the constant streams of dragons that had arrived attempting to peer inside Kiara's cave and make a guess at what was wrong with her egg. As guardian of her and her new hatchling his job was harder than for others. But he puffed out his chest. He was determined not to let Kiara and Ketu down.

"Be careful little hatchlings," he said, leaning down so his large face was level with their small ones. The bravest Talana shrunk back, giggling nervously. "I am here to protect this cave and see that Kiara is not disturbed from tending to her new born when the egg hatches. I should not think twice about gobbling up any little intruders."

With that he snapped his mouth as the three dragons raced back down the hill, shrieking with terror.

Grinning to himself Romao watched the Talanas run away, but the smile soon fell from his face. Dragor clans generally disliked and suspected one another, and whilst these little dragons caused no harm, he could not be so sure about some of their elders. The purple Alanas argued constantly with the red Nephans and held a longstanding bitterness towards them. There was also a general disharmony in Dragor, and the stories were spreading thick and fast that something should be done about the Nephan clan egg. Romao hoped the night would be over before anything bad happened. The guards were never usually needed but tonight he was keeping a tight hold of his spear.

He gazed out from the cave to where the steaming mud pools joined with The Fire and then across the great waters to the view of the tallest of all their mountains. He considered how it stood proudly as though it was acting as the Dragor guardian itself. A sudden noise alerted him to the approach of Yula, the Hudrah. She was heaving her great bulk down the stony path and puffing determinedly. He watched as she came closer, wondering if now was the time for Kiara's egg to crack.

Yula had been the Hudrah of the Nephan clan since anyone could remember, and like all Hudrahs her life was shrouded in mystery. These female dragons were self appointed by a special talent they discovered, and each clan had its own Hudrah who lived on the charity of their dragons for every day of the year except for one. On New Birth's Eve she would throw her black wicker basket over her shoulder, don her silver cape, and leave to preside over the hatching. Without the work of dragons like Yula, dragon-kind would die out in a few generations. She and the rest of her kind were treated with the utmost respect and looked forward to being rewarded for this night's special duties. Superstition held that should a dragon be cursed by the words of a Hudrah then they would bear a curse for as long as they walked so most were very eager to please them.

Other dragons in Dragor laboured in the skilled work

of their various clans such as artistry, fishing and mining, and the other unofficial role of the Hudrah was to ensure younger dragons kept to their proper work. With every generation it seemed the younger dragons thought they would be better placed to try out the tasks of a different clan, and had to be persuaded back to the right path.

"Look at your small claws, your blunted nose, your soft little ears," Yula had chided a small Nephan dragon only a week ago for his ambitions to be a fishing-dragon. "You do not have the fast eyesight of the Alana clan, the large wings for stamina in the skies, or the pointed snout for turning out the fish, so you should not hope to join them when they fly to the bay of The Great Waters, for you will never bring a catch as they do."

Hudrahs also often solved arguments between the clans who generally only liked to be with their own kind. They fell outside this general practice and formed friendships between one another so were often best placed to make decisions over many matters where other dragons couldn't get along. Some said they possessed the sharpest of hearing which enabled them to hear the tiniest crack in the shell of an egg, whilst others thought it was the blue stones they wore around their necks that held magical powers and seemed to glow stronger to foretell a new life. Romao noticed that Yula's blue stone sparkled in the falling light of the dusk as she moved slowly up the mountain.

Whatever their secret the Hudrah was always present at each and every birth to perfect timing. For a brief moment Romao thought that the birth had come already, and long before he had checked that Ketu had prepared the sorrel juice.

But it was only early evening, and Romao reminded himself he had a long time to wait and that Yula must be coming because she wanted something. This was the part of his guarding post which was the hardest – remaining patient into the long night. He looked on keenly as Yula came closer.

It was a fearful legend of Dragor that as well as watching over the birth, the Hudrah would take away any new dragon that proved too sickly to continue life in their clan. It had never happened in Romao's lifetime, and only a handful of older dragons claimed that the black wicker basket had been used on New Birth's Eve. And so over time this function of the Hudrah had become more of a myth than a reality. But it didn't stop Romao peeking to see if he could catch a glimpse of it beneath the silver cape. He could see nothing, however, below the glittering fabric.

Yula was carrying a bowl of sweet sticky mash with a small silver spoon. She panted as she trod the final dusty path up to the cave, and handed Romao the luscious-smelling food.

"Take it, take it," she wheezed. "It does me good to see the young dragons eat." And she sat down to catch her breath.

Romao took a spoonful respectfully and thanked her. Yula made some of the best sticky mash of anyone in the

Nephan clan.

"Do you know of any unnusualness with the egg?" she asked immediately, peering into the gloom of the cave. "Does Kiara move from her nest?"

"I do not know Yula," said Romao, only half truthfully, realising that she was trying to bribe him for information. He had gone into the cave only once to greet Kiara and Ketu and reassure them that he intended to do the very best as their guard. He had at this time judged for himself by the small remains of quartz nest that Kiara had made it her only meal since she had settled on it many moons ago. But this was a fact he didn't think necessary to share with any outsiders.

The older dragon had a ridge of worry etched into her thick scales that Romao had never seen before, and he realised that Yula was actually nervous. The thought made him worry in turn. What should a Hudrah with over a hundred winters have to fear on New Birth's Eve?

She seemed to sense his thoughts and sat up again, picking at the ground with her scaly claw as if unconcerned. "No matter Romao, I shall know soon enough," she said, eyeing into the cave one last time. And with that she unfolded her vast dusty wings and flung herself with surprising speed from the mountain top. Romao watched as she dipped and then rose unsteadily into the darkening sky.

"It was the only sound they spoke, and most dragons thought The Ageless Ones were simply witless, their placid faces giving nothing away."

Chapter Two

The Ageless Ones

Yula had been gone for several hours and Romao was wearing thin the scales on his feet, tramping the dusty earth outside the cave. He didn't know how much longer it would be until the hatching, but as a loyal Guard Dragon he would wait until dawn.

Romao pricked up his ears as a crash from inside the cave echoed out. But the noise was soon followed by the smell of sorrel juice and Ketu's low voice.

"Not to worry Romao!" he shouted. "Clumsy claws has dropped a bowl of sorrel juice."

In a moment Ketu was at the entrance, his frame filling it almost entirely. "I am sorry if we have neglected you," he said, clearly in good spirits despite the gossip surrounding his mate. "Kiara keeps to her nest and it makes extra work for me. Not that I mind," he added quickly. "But I do not find it as easy to make a cauldron of sorrel juice as most, and I have just tipped my last attempt all over the cave floor."

Ketu eyed the rows of footprints on the ground. There were dozens of them, all the shapes and sizes of the different dragons who'd come to find out more about the egg. His voice dropped to a whisper. "There are still rumours that something is not right?" said Ketu. He didn't

17

need to say what he was talking about.

Romao nodded, not sure whether he should be embarrassed in front of Ketu at the attention their egg was attracting.

To his surprise Ketu did not go back into the cave, but instead sat easily on his haunches, motioning Romao to do the same. They sat in companionable silence for a moment before Ketu laid a kindly claw on his arm.

"You do not fear then?" he said. "For the egg?"

Romao didn't know how to answer such a direct question. But instead of waiting for an answer Ketu smiled reassuringly and spoke again.

"Of course you must Romao," he continued. "You must not be afraid that I shall be insulted. I know all that the clans are saying, and it is only natural that someone on his first guard duty should overhear things. But you should not worry. The other kinds of dragon don't trust the Nephans any more than we trust them. Those who are not of our clan will say anything to make themselves feel like they are the best kind of dragon there is, and are happy to spread silly things."

Ketu looked across to decide whether Romao had confidence in his words and patted his arm again. "I will tell you a story," he said. "Of many months past when you had only just won our guardship, and Kiara was at her nest for the first time." he looked at Romao to check he was ready to hear the tale.

"Do you know of The Ageless Ones?" he began.

Romao nodded, and he leaned forward to hear more.

The Ageless Ones were twin dragons of the Saiga clan. The two dragonesses were the deep indigo blue of their fellow clan members, but unlike other Saigas their faces were almost perfectly smooth and expressionless, with opal-coloured eyes. They wore special stones around their necks that seemed to swirl with mystical colours and patterns, and the Hudrah, who knew about such things, swore that these stones gave out a strange energy. Nothing else of their past was known, not even their age, which was why they were known as The Ageless Ones.

Even more mysteriously, any attempt to communicate with them was met with either silence, or a dual chorus of a strange sound, and for this reason they were also known as 'The Yeahs'. Certain questions, or the right time of year, could prompt them to take a deep breath in tandem, and then huff out a steady tune of "yeeeeaaahh".

It was the only sound they spoke, and most dragons thought The Ageless Ones were simply witless, their placid faces giving nothing away, their conversation limited to a single word that had no meaning to anyone.

Seeing Romao's interest, Ketu drew himself up a little taller. "It was a time of great worry for Kiara and I, Romao, for the egg had been laid and the talking of the clans began almost immediately."

Romao nodded again, noting that Ketu neither confirmed nor denied that there was a reason for his egg to create the interest it did.

"I was in the Saiga village," he continued. "Buying some herbs and potions, for Kiara loves to be prepared,

19

and she wanted to be sure she had every medicine for the cave. But I was weighed down with cares. Without thinking I sat down in front of The Ageless Ones to sort through my basket. When I looked up they were staring down at me. It was no different from how they usually gaze out blankly at the market place – it is very hard to tell from their eyes if anything is going on – but I had a feeling somehow, as though some kind of connection had been made."

He looked at Romao, as if wondering whether his story would be believed.

"I found myself pouring out my whole story," he said. "Of how Kiara's chest had begun to speckle, and of how overjoyed we were to be bringing forth a new hatchling. Then I explained about you, and how it made us both even happier to have such a strong young guard to protect our cave."

Romao tucked his head down modestly, but could not hide his pleasure. He too had hoped for the honour of guarding Ketu and Kiara.

"Then I told them of all the rumours and of our fears for the egg," said Ketu now keeping his eyes fixed to the dusty floor. "I talked of how I had to reassure Kiara of our hatchling's health when I did not feel the certainty myself, and that with many moons left to go I feared I would not have the strength to continue comforting her without more confidence."

Romao was silent. It had never occurred to him that Ketu, well known in the clan for his courage, had been so troubled.

"Then a strange thing happened," said Ketu. "The Ageless Ones leaned forward and firmly took my arms."

Romao gasped. Never in all the clans had the twin dragons been known to communicate in such a manner with another dragon though many had tried talking to them. He studied Ketu carefully wondering what to make of the story.

"I felt as though I were being pulled into another place, another time," he continued. "It was as if the whole of Dragor was rushing away from me. And then, just as suddenly I saw myself, a few winters older, with a young dragon at my side. I knew instinctively that this was my son. That is when I knew, Romao, that all would be well."

He stood to leave, his account over, and Romao scrambled up beside him.

"And, The Ageless Ones?" he asked. "They have not... You have not been to them since?" Romao was wondering if Ketu had some special quality to unlock the power of these twins.

"Many times," said Ketu. "I walk past them often, and still stop to talk to them. But never again have they blessed me with a vision." He stopped as if considering something. "I believe, without doubt, they have powers which are not known elsewhere in Dragor," he said. "Some ancient knowledge that we may come to know of in time." And then he turned and tracked back into the cave.

Romao gazed out through the smoking mud pools into the distance. It was night now, and the heavy dark had rolled in. He had been taught at school that beyond Dragor, far up in the night sky hung balls of flaming gas that lit the sky, even when the sun set. These sky-fires were said to be hidden from view by the mists of the mud pools and the smoke from The Fire Which Must Never Go Out. He wondered what it might be like to fly from Dragor and see such sights. But it was law that no-one was allowed to leave their land. Since dragons had escaped humans it was too dangerous to return.

As he let his imagination roam past the borders of the clans Romao heard a familiar sound. Yula was puffing up the mountain again, but this time she looked more intent than he had ever seen her. And then echoing out from the cave came a tremendous crack, like the branch of a tree breaking.

His stomach lurched. This must be it, he realised. The hatching was about the take place.

From inside the cave he heard Kiara gasp. And then Ketu called.

"Romao. Is Yula here? The egg is hatching!"

"She is almost to the top of the mountain," called Romao. And he rushed down to help the old dragon to the top.

"It is time" said Romao, as he took her arm. But she shook off his hand gruffly. "I heard it," said Yula. "No dragon could miss that sound. Hudrah or not."

But she had not been in the cave when the egg had first broken, Romao realised. For the first time in dragon history a Hudrah had not foretold the birth. It had come

22

slightly earlier than she had expected, and now she would be late in administering the first blessing to the hatchling.

As they entered the cave Ketu and Kiara were perched wordlessly in front of their egg, their eyes shining.

But Yula and Romao stopped sharp in the doorway. The older dragon's eyes widened in amazement, and Romao realised in a moment that the rumours had been true.

Healthy dragon eggs were a delicate lilac colour, which fell in pretty shards around the pale new hatchling, Dragon parents often talked with pleasure of how beautiful their new born looked, soft pink before their clan colours had deepened, and perfectly matching the fragments of shell.

This egg was different. It was every colour of the rainbow.

The shell was jewelled like the contents of a treasure chest and vivid with vibrant swirls of turquoise, green, scarlet and violet. It shone and sparkled in the firelight. To Romao it looked like a precious and wonderful thing.

"Come closer Romao," said Kiara, her face alive with the excitement of the moment. "The crack is widening."

Romao moved to approach the egg, but Yula shouldered him roughly aside.

"A guard should not be in the cave," she announced roughly. "It is bad luck for the hatchling. Have him wait outside and do his duty."

But Ketu was not about to see his mate disagreed with.

"Romao is a friend as well as a guard." he beckoned the young dragon over. "Step forward Romao, we should like you to share in our joy."

Yula's face hardened but she said nothing. And then as they watched, the crack began to open. It split into three sections, then eight, and finally they could just see a determined little snout tapping away at the shell.

Kiara breathed out in relief. The hatchling was the same soft pink of all dragon newborns.

Pieces of the shell began to fall away, and the tiny dragon was left with an unwieldy piece of its former home covering its head.

Kiara moved forward to nudge it off with her nose, but Yula stepped forward to stop her.

"Let the hatchling forge his own path," she cried. "The newborn must make the journey unaided to the Land of Dragor. Otherwise it may not be strong enough to survive the tests of its first three winters.

She withdrew a sheaf of herbs and began mumbling a blessing. Ketu and Kiara exchanged glances, but made no further move to help their hatchling. And to their great relief the shell fell away suddenly, revealing all of their newborn with his soft scales and miniature claws.

Kiara scooped him up in great delight and nuzzled the little dragon.

"Isn't he perfect?" she asked, holding him out to the others. "See his straight muzzle, his big sparkly green eyes and lovely ears?"

Ketu took up the new born, filled with pride. "Our beautiful son," he said holding him aloft and then bringing the baby close back against his chest.

"What shall you call him Kiara?" asked Romao, looking to the mother, whose joy it was to name her hatchling.

Kiara blinked happily. "Yoshiko," she said. "His name shall be Yoshiko." And she leaned forward to kiss the newly-named hatchling.

But as she did so a great cry went up from outside the cave. Romao turned in alarm, stepping forward protectively to the entrance.

Gathered around the doorway was a cluster of dragon elders from various clans, and Romao recognised Gandar at their head. He was a sly-looking Alana dragon who was well known for being lazy and letting his mate Agna do all the work.

Tonight Agna was expecting her own hatching to take place, and it was typical that Gandar didn't seem to feel he should be with her, helping. Instead he was causing trouble for other clans.

"We have all heard the rumours Romao," announced Gandar loudly. "The egg is cursed. We must take the hatchling away before it brings harm to Dragor."

Romao's face darkened. "You have your own hatchling to attend to Gandar," he said. "You should be with your mate, looking to your own business."

"I am here to protect Dragor," said Gandar. "The new hatchling could be a threat. We must take him to the Council and have him assessed there."

Romao stood bodily in front of the cave and stared down at the little group. "You'll have to come past me," he said evenly, setting his feet firmly on the floor.

Gandar gritted his teeth, obviously weighing up the threat.

"Move aside Romao," he said. "It is for the good of Dragor."

"My guard duty is sacred to me," said Romao. "If I have to battle every dragon here, you will not enter the cave."

The assembled dragons were clearly becoming less certain, as if it had not already occurred to them that crossing the threshold of the cave and taking the hatchling might be a problem. Already some were starting to shuffle their feet as if they'd rather be elsewhere.

Gandar noticed the mood, and glowered at Romao. "I will not forget this!" he hissed. "You have endangered our great land tonight!" And with a sweep of his great wings he turned and flew off into the night. Behind him the other dragons launched hastily after him.

Romao returned into the cave, but nothing prepared him for the drama unfolding inside.

Whilst he had been defending Kiara and Ketu from Gandar and the other Alanas, Yula had done the unthinkable. There was a flash of black and gasps of horror. For the first time in her history as a Hudrah,

Yula had taken out the black wicker basket. Romao's eyes widened and Ketu moved instinctively to protect Kiara and his new baby dragon.

"What do you mean by it Yula?" he exclaimed. "Our hatchling is well and healthy."

But Yula shook her head slowly. "Step aside Ketu," she said. "Do not obstruct the Hudrah in her work. You heard the dragons outside. The hatchling is cursed. Any dragon who saw the shell would know this. It is my duty to protect the clans."

Kiara wrapped the tiny bundle even tighter in her arms and set her jaw defiantly. "There is nothing wrong with this dragon," she said. "Any who looked at him would know he is a blessed creature, finely formed and healthy. It is only sick dragons who may be carried away by the..." but she could not bring herself to say the words.

Romao was held transfixed by the dark object. It looked more like a pouch than a basket, but there was no mistaking the ancient wickerwork.

"The black wicker basket is for the good of all the clans," said Yula smoothly. "Give me the dragon Kiara, or I shall use Hudrah powers to take him from you. Once the basket has emerged there is no hope for the sickly one."

Kiara and Ketu exchanged fearful glances, but it was Romao who stepped forward, taking Yula calmly by the shoulder. "It has been a long night Ma'am" he said. "Thirteen births so far and this your fourteenth."

Yula nodded uncertainly.

"The dragon is as well made as any healthy young hatchling," continued Romao. "None could say there is anything flawed in him. And as for the shell, it is only the firelight that makes it glint strangely."

Seizing the moment Ketu stepped forward. "It is late and we are all tired Yula," he agreed. "And I have not yet paid you for your services." Taking out a purse he counted out twenty glass stones and pressed them meaningfully into Yula's hand.

The old dragon's claw held open for a moment as she looked down in wonder at the money. It was more than ten times what she had expected to be paid for the entire night. Her breath slowed as she considered. True enough, she thought that there was nothing physically wrong with the dragon, besides it being born of such an unusual egg shell. But now she looked again, perhaps it was a trick of light. Inch by inch her yellowed talons closed around the stones.

Ketu breathed a sigh of relief as Yula slid the black wicker basket away under her cape and pulled out instead the large birthing book. She thumbed to a new page.

"Name of hatchling?" she asked, hefting a thick charcoal pen.

"Yoshiko." Kiara and Ketu hardly dared look at one another.

"Distinguishing features?"

"None," said Ketu firmly.

Yula carefully recorded the details of the newborn and his parentage into her book. "Perhaps he will be a little warrior like his namesake," she murmured, looking to where Yoshiko's tiny snout was now snuffling the warm air of the cave. But Kiara wasn't listening. She was stroking delightedly at her newborn.

Yula stood to leave and Romao rose to exit with her, but when they reached the entrance of the cave Ketu drew him back.

"We are in your debt Romao," he said, as they watched Yula take flight in the direction of the Alana clan. "We nearly lost our hatchling and had it not been for your intervention I do not know if Yula would have changed her mind."

Romao nodded, but neither made any mention of the black wicker basket. The night had been hard enough already.

"The cauldron of sage juice tumbled to the floor spilling the green liquid, and the echoes of Agna's wail rang long and deep through the mountain."

Chapter Three

Igorr

As dawn broke Yula flew purposefully over Dragor watching the dragons beneath her change colours with each clan land she passed. She turned left over the rugged mountains of the Talana clan, where the blue dragons were burrowing into the hillside with grunts, and rounded on the lush hills of the Effram clan, where the green dragons were using their skill as artists to make colourful pots and paintings.

Finally the caves began to show purple – Alana dragons who were packing up nets for the day's fishing. Yula landed unsteadily at the entrance to Agna and Gandar's cave, where Setu was barely keeping his eyes open. Unlike Romao he'd had to fetch and carry all night to make up for Agna's absent mate, and was so tired he could barely do his guard duty.

The Alana clan had a Hudrah called Pp who had watched over their newborn for as long as anyone could remember, and Yula had flown towards their waterside homes hoping to find her friend finished for the night. But as she landed Setu was still in his guarding position.

"The egg has not yet begun to crack," he explained. Before he could guide Yula to the entrance a sharp voice echoed out.

"Is she here Setu?" asked Agna, hearing Yula arrive. "Send her in but be sure you do not come too close to the cave. I would not have my young hatchling soured by bad luck." Agna like Yula, claimed it was unlucky for any Guard Dragon to see an egg crack on New Birth's Eve. Usually this was a superstition of the eldest clan members and Agna was still a young dragon. Setu therefore suspected Agna kept it only to lord her importance over him like a lowly servant.

"She'll need all the luck she can get," he muttered to himself "with her egg not even cracked by dawn on New Birth's Eve and her mate nowhere to be seen."

As usual Gandar was absent, though the morning mists had almost begun to rise and all the other births of the night had already taken place.

But in reply Setu raised his voice and called: "It is the Nephan clan Hudrah, she has come hoping the egg is already hatched and she can go with Pp to register the births." The resentment in his voice was obvious. The presence of the father was known to hasten the hatching, and in Gandar's absence Setu had been subjected to a longer wait. In the sky above he could just make out a speck of a purple dragon getting larger and larger. At first he thought it could be Gandar, returned to do his duty. But he quickly realised it was Pp flying high in the distance. His heart leapt knowing that her arrival should spell the end of his long wait.

Pp landed, her dusty scales settling heavily next to

Setu. She nodded at the other Hudrah, pleased to see her friend, and tapped the blue stone around her neck, eyeing Yula knowingly.

"Not yet close to hatching and I'll bet I know why," she said. Gandar's fickle nature was talked of in all the clans. "Come Yula. Perhaps the two of us can tempt this new dragon to hatch" and she gestured her friend to follow her inside the cave.

"It is better that Gandar is not here," Agna's justification drifted out of the cave entrance as Yula and Pp entered. "He will be such a doting father but he is a free spirit who needs time to think on New Birth's Eve."

But the Nephan Hudrah was not to be deterred. "It is irregular that the father is not present at the birth," she scolded. "Pp needs both elders present to record the details."

Agna grunted in surprise. "I heard it was once allowed at another birth." She said as she looked across at Pp pleadingly. Pp sighed, but Yula folded her arms crossly. Then before any reply could be made a tiny tentative crack was heard.

"He is hatching!" cried Agna, rushing to where the thinnest of hairline breaks had appeared in the shell. "It must be a boy dragon I am sure of it. That is what Gandar forecast. A strong male."

The thin crack had split open wide now, and a tiny slick slice of a blackish purple could be seen inside the egg. The scales were so small that they almost merged into one, and Agna held her breath.

The little face of the dragon had the long snout of the Alana clan, perfect for pulling fish from the waters of Dragor, but it was shorter than usual and the eyes were narrowed. As the dragon emerged looking stern and angry it became obvious from his eye shape he was a male hatchling.

"He seems annoyed at something," said Pp almost laughing, but Yula felt discomforted by the rage that seemed to be radiating off the newborn. Agna, however, scooped up the young dragon and held him proudly aloft.

"We have a warrior," she announced, her eyes glittering with triumph. "A warrior son for Gandar. See already that his scales are strong and his claws sharp". And she tapped the needle-like talons of the newborn.

Suddenly Agna let out a strange howl, causing Yula to jump and Setu to call nervously from the outside of the cave.

"What is it Pp" he shouted. "Something is wrong?"

But before either of them could answer Agna had risen to her hind legs, flailing her wings wildly in the small confines of the cave. The cauldron of sage juice tumbled to the floor spilling the green liquid, and the echoes of Agna's wail rang long and deep through the mountain.

"My son!" she announced again. "Igorr! All of you who have doubted Gandar and I shall regret your judgements. This dragon will win us many honours."

34

And she raised Igorr even higher, his look of fury glowering over the two Hudrahs.

It was Yula who first broke the spell of Agna's odd behaviour, stepping forward and taking the dragon gently from her talons.

"You must have your mate in the cave before you celebrate," she said. "As I have said already, not even his name can be recorded until Gandar is here. You are too quick to be triumphant Agna."

But the younger female seemed to be in some kind of trance as she handed Igorr over for Pp to inspect.

Eventually Gandar arrived to acknowledge the birth of his son. He stayed only long enough to gobble down the feast that Agna had earlier prepared for him, then made some excuse and flew off again into the night.

The two Hudrahs had so much to gossip over when they finally left the cave that they almost forgot about the strange business of Kiara's egg.

"Perhaps after all these years it's Gandar we should feel sorry for rather than Agna," said Pp, and they both shuffled back down the mountain. "Whilst he may not be responsible at least he is in charge of his senses."

Yula shuddered, thinking back to the crazed Agna.

"But you did not tell me of Kiara's egg," continued her friend. "Did you use the basket as you said you would?" Like most Hudrahs Pp hoped to mark out her time in Dragor never having to use the dreaded basket, but its use still held a huge fascination for her. "I judged the dragon to be healthy," Yula replied keeping her reply to a minimum.

"But the egg? It was normal then? Not a curse on Dragor?"

Yula coughed uncomfortably. "There was nothing strange about the egg," she said. "A trick of the firelight, that was all. Some passing dragons must have seen the sorrel juice reflected on the egg and thought it to be patterned or some such." She didn't mention that she was one of those dragons.

Pp eyed her friend curiously. "Of course I always thought it was nonsense that the egg might be square-shaped," she said carefully. "And every Hudrah knows that a dragon egg cannot sing from inside. These are all silly tales. But I had a thought to myself Yula, like all the clans who were thinking the same thing, that perhaps it was a coloured egg."

Yula froze, and Pp continued talking, pretending she hadn't noticed the other Hudrah's face.

"Of course every dragon, even the very little hatchlings, know of what happened the last time a coloured egg was laid." she said. "Surion was born, and with his gift of fire the dragons went to battle with the humans."

"Yes yes," said Yula angrily. "The red egg. The birth of Surion. Who doesn't know that tale? Every little dragon in Fire School learns it."

"There is no need to get angry," said Pp. "I am just thinking aloud as to what it might mean if another egg

36

of that kind is hatched. After all, the birth of Surion is the legend of Dragor itself. But it was so long ago – and who can claim to have all the true facts about what happened before Dragor? Before we were all hidden from humans in our land of smoke and mist? No dragon is old enough. For all we know another red egg could mean the end of Dragor."

She paused, as if choosing her words, and continued "No dragon really knows what happened do they Yula? Still. It would be strange wouldn't it? If another red egg came to Dragor after all this time. Born again to a Nephan dragon."

Yula looked Pp straight in the eye. "You are talking nonsense like any other Alana," she said. "I can assure you Pp the egg was not red. It was no Surion egg."

The two Hudrahs continued their journey in silence, both with their own thoughts.

There was great argument amongst the clans as to whether the red egg born in the time of humans had been a blessing or a curse. Those with younglings recognised the huge blessing their escape yielded, as in those times their baby dragons were taken from them and sold by the humans to be slaves. Yula, however, who had no family, shared the negative perspective. In her mind escaping from man had bought a whole heap of problems that didn't exist before. The clans had been forced into hiding, using their skills to keep a fire burning to shield them from the prying eyes of man. Since that time the dragons had lived in discontent and disharmony, missing their true native lands, and bickering with one another.

But if Surion's red egg had been a curse what did a multicoloured dragon egg mean for the clans? Yula had already begun to regret her decision not to take the hatchling away. Thinking back she became all the more certain that her eyes didn't deceive her. Kiara must be watched.

"Shivering in the cool of the night
Kiara gently unwrapped the
cloth and let the glittering pieces of
the egg tumble free."

Chapter Four

Hiding the Egg

Kiara hardly dared breathe. Tired from the drama of New Birth's Eve Ketu had fallen into a deep sleep, and the tiny Yoshiko lay by his side, rasping out gentle snores. She gazed at him adoringly, his tiny wings impossibly perfect, and his soft scales not yet hardened by the fire games.

She gave him an experimental lick to check he was soundly asleep, and then as slowly as she was able, eased herself from the nest. Lying on the cave floor were the bright fragments of Yoshiko's egg and she gathered them quickly and carefully, taking care to make as little noise as possible.

Memories of the black wicker basket still gripped her stomach tightly. For a few brief moments she thought she would lose her newborn, and she marvelled that it had taken only seconds of him being born to make this the most terrifying event of her life.

Yula, she knew, still suspected something was not right with the egg. And whilst the black basket could not now re-emerge and the birth had been logged, she was still nervous that the old dragon could make trouble for her perfect hatchling.

Yula could go to Kinga thought Kiara, imagining

the great Nephan leader sitting firm on his throne of treasure, with Yula showing him the glittering broken shell of the egg. Kinga might decree that Yoshiko be taken away and raised under supervision. Even the thought of it made her tremble.

Still shaking slightly she packed up the pieces into a wide cloth, and threw it onto her back. Then she crept out of the cave and down the mountain. Only at the bottom did she spread her wings and beat the air into powerful waves which propelled her upwards into the skies of Dragor.

Turning on the wind she steadied herself with her tail and headed to a part of the dragon lands where few ever went. The villages grew small beneath her and the general festivities of New Birth's Eve quietened as she flew further and further from civilisation, towards the dragon's graveyard.

Legend had it that the mystical place saw the bones of the dragons rise up once a year, armed with magical weapons that, if witnessed, would render any of the Guard Dragons invincible. And every summertime the young hopefuls would descend on the graveyard to honour their ancestors, bringing beautiful flowers that the Mida Clan farming dragons had grown, and throw colourful parties to ask for the spirit of these special gifts.

But this night was different. Kiara landed on the barren-looking stretch of land, remembering when she'd first come here as a younger dragon, excited by the herald of the moon, and drawn to the carnival atmosphere. No-one came here in darkness for any other reason than to die.

Her heart hammering in her chest Kiara eyed the landscape. In this part of Dragor the veil of smoke separating the human and dragon world was at its thinnest.

Shivering in the cool of the night Kiara gently unwrapped the cloth and let the glittering pieces of the egg tumble free. Then, looking guiltily around, she drew in a deep breath and blew out a thick tunnel of flame. It roared around the eggshell in a fierce red heat, and when she'd finished with everything in her lungs Kiara looked back down, expecting to see nothing but ash.

To her amazement the shell sat perfectly, as if nothing had happened. She prodded it experimentally with her claw. It wasn't even hot.

Confused, Kiara raised her foot, and pounded down onto the shell as hard as she could, twisting and crushing it into the hard ground. When she drew up her claws the pieces were not even scratched.

She eyed them hesitantly, wondering what to do next. Then Kiara began to dig a little hole in the sandy earth, and as she worked steadily it became deeper and wider. She thought she heard something on the breeze and was startled. She looked over her shoulder suspiciously yet there appeared to be nothing. Just her and the colourful shell.

Dropping the pieces into the ground she looked at them sadly for one long last time. Kiara knew it was the eyes of a loving mother looking at the shell, but she deeply wished she could keep it as most parents did, placing it safe in a gilded box for their young dragons to marvel at when they were old enough. She remembered herself as a young dragon. Did I really come from there mummy? And a little tear came, thinking Yoshiko would always be different. And with a determined puff she scooped the dull grey earth over the sparkling fragments, blotting out their bright colours forever.

Kiara had hoped her heart would lift as she took off again for the skies, leaving the evidence of the egg safely concealed where no dragon could ever find it. But something troubled her. Something she couldn't quite put her talon on.

Back in the dragon's graveyard two yellow eyes blinked against the dark night. Yula watched Kiara grow smaller and smaller, and then spread her own wings.

"One of these spirits is a
great snake, whose belly forms a
long wide gully, and whose
head is a rock as wide as all The
Great Waters of Dragor and the
colour of fire"

Chapter Five

Myths and Legends

New Birth's Eve turned to Green Earth Night, Yellow Harvest became Red Seventh Moon, and before Kiara and Ketu knew it Yoshiko had weathered four winters.

Other dragon clans almost came to forget the mysterious circumstances of his birth, and since that fateful night Yula had kept her lips tightly sealed, refusing to tell even the other Hudrahs that anything strange had occurred.

Only Kiara noticed that sometimes, when the sun was low, Yoshiko's vibrant red colour could take on a different tone. Like a soft pink, or a dusky violet. But since the change was so tiny no other dragon paid attention. Dragor was a land of colours, after all, with each dragon clan boasting a bright bold shade.

Ketu loved to tell Yoshiko the dramatic story of his birth, drawing his wings wide to emphasise the black wicker basket, and making the terrifying object bigger and bigger to his son's delight.

"Was it as big as this cave?" asked Yoshiko, his eyes gleaming.

"Much bigger," said Ketu. "And the colour was the darkest black you've ever seen."

"And then Yula changed her mind?" This was

Yoshiko's favourite part of the story.

"When she saw your little snout and tiny claws she announced you the most perfect little dragon she'd ever seen," said Ketu. "And she hadn't the heart to carry you away."

"Tell me what really happened!" demanded Yoshiko, as this had become part of the game he played with his father. Ketu pretended to sigh as if the truth was being dragged out of him.

"Alright alright I'll tell you." he said. "But you must promise not to get frightened." He eyed Kiara who seemed otherwise occupied on the far side of the cave. She was blowing fire onto a wooden canvas to make a picture for the inside of the cave.

Yoshiko nodded expectantly.

"The basket was full of terrible ghouls and monsters," said Ketu, as Yoshiko squeaked in terror. "And flesh-eating bats and ugly spiders who scuttled out to try and drag you in with them. Some were as big as a Talana elder, and others crawled over the floor. Clinging things and things that scuttled, with claws and legs and eyes and teeth!"

"Tell me what happened next?" Yoshiko bounced impatiently.

"The monsters heard a great cry, and saw the fearsome dragon Yoshiko," said Ketu. "And though you were only a small hatchling when they laid eyes on you for the first time they all ran away in fear!"

Kiara looked up from her picture, which though

she wasn't an artist like an Effram dragon, was taking shape nicely. "Time for some different stories," she said. "Tell him the story of the Bushki clan." And Ketu rolled his eyes and settled himself to explain.

"Do you know why the Bushki dragons have such a sweet tooth?" he asked. Yoshiko shook his head. "Then I will tell you," said Ketu.

"A long long time ago, before dragons lived together they were scattered all over the earth," he paused to see if Yoshiko was listening. "That's why all the clans have their own different gifts. The purple Alanas are fisherfolk, and the blue Talanas dig under the earth with their powerful horns, and the Nephans..."

"We are the leaders!" interrupted Yoshiko, flapping his wings up and down in excitement. "And we are the best of the best clan!"

"Not the best," corrected Ketu. "The red Nephans solve problems and lead other dragons on important matters. But without the Alanas there would be no fish for your Red Seventh Moon Stew, and without the Talanas we wouldn't have our fine deep caves to live in."

He paused, remembering himself. "But I was telling you the story of the yellow Bushki clan, and how they came to like all sweet things," he said.

"The Bushkis run the book-houses," said Yoshiko with certainty. "Kiara told me."

"Not just the book-houses," said Ketu. "They keep all the records of the clans since the beginning of Dragor, and record every new birth and every history."

"What came before Dragor?" asked Yoshiko.

"That's a story you'll learn when you go to school," said Ketu. "And most likely it will be a book from a Bushki dragon where you'll read about it. It's a very serious history of Surion, our great leader who lead the dragons to victory."

He leaned over to tickle Yoshiko's tail. "Do you want me to tell you the story of the Buskhi clan? Or would you like to crush the sorrel for the sorrel juice instead?"

Yoshiko made a face and Ketu laughed.

"The Bushki clan come from a land far far away," he began. "Whilst Dragor is cool and full of mountains, Bushki country is dry and hot, and yellow all over just like the dragons. It is a place of powerful spirits who lie sleeping the long length of the land."

"One of these spirits is a great snake, whose belly forms a long wide gully, and whose head is a rock as wide as all the Great Waters of Dragor and the colour of fire," said Ketu, pausing to point to Kiara's steady flame for effect.

"One day the sun was particularly fierce, and the day especially dry and the snake was basking lazily in the heat. From the swirl of his dreams came creatures of bright colours, and they walked two by two into the hot sun."

Yoshiko blinked in wonder, imagining the animals coming fully formed from the imagination of a great spirit.

"Animals of all shapes and sizes came walking out into the hot sand, but biggest of all were the Bushki dragons, and they shone yellow like sunshine itself. But there was nothing for the dragons to eat, and the snake, seeing his mistake woke drowsily from his slumber and looked around the barren land. Then he thumped his great tail three times. Thump! Thump! Thump! And from the ground rose up toffee-nut trees like those you see in Dragor."

"Is that why the Bushki love the toffee-nuts?" asked Yoshiko, and Ketu nodded.

"The Bushki are not farmers like the Mida clan, and they cannot make beautiful pots like the Effram dragons. But they are the only ones who can make the toffee-nuts grow, and without them there would be no sweet nuts at Yellow Harvest."

Yoshiko gave this some thought. "Tell me the story of Surion!" he insisted, unwilling to forget his earlier request. He loved to hear Ketu telling stories, but so far his elders had managed to avoid telling him Dragor's most important legend. Apparently it was too warlike for a young dragon, but Yoshiko was convinced he was old enough to hear it.

Ketu's eyes slid over to Kiara who seemed occupied in her picture-making, and let his voice lower again to a dramatic whisper.

"Alright I'll tell you the story," he agreed. "But all the dragon clans tell it slightly differently. So you must promise me that you won't show up at Fire School and disagree with your teacher when she tells you it."

Yoshiko bobbed his head solemnly.

"Well then," said Ketu, settling lower on his haunches for effect. "This was how it was."

"A long, long time ago. Long before you were born, or I was born, or many dragons before us, the clans lived with humans in the world beyond Dragor."

Yoshiko's eyes grew round. "What are humans?"

"They are a special species like dragons," explained Ketu. "They have the ability to make enchantments and share thoughts through talking just as we do. But they are a dark kind of creature, and they do not always use their powers for good. And when dragons walked the earth with humans, they tricked us into being their slaves."

"What's a slave?" asked Yoshiko.

"It is when someone has no freedom of their own, but must work all the time at another's choosing," said Ketu. "We were slaves to the humans, and they used us to ride them around the sky, and to carry heavy things for them, for humans are not strong in their bodies like dragons."

"But why didn't we just fly away?" asked Yoshiko, trying to imagine how the mighty dragons could ever be held captives by such a weak sounding species.

"The humans are very clever," said Ketu. "They knew of special herbs which they put in our food, and with these they kept us sleepy and drugged. Then one day a special egg was born."

"Surion!" Breathed Yoshiko. Every dragon had heard of Surion.

"Yes," said Ketu. "Surion of the red egg. At first when the egg came to his dragon elder the others were afraid. They thought it brought a curse." he stopped for a moment as if about to say more to his young son, and then shaking his head he continued with the story.

"But the egg did not bring a curse," he said firmly. "It brought a dragon who could instinctively breathe fire. He did not have to be taught as other dragons do, and he gave this skill to all the clans. Then using the fire we were able to escape the humans."

"Surion's father Goadah was himself a great warrior, and between them they helped organise the clans to break their bonds and escape. Together they flew all over the world teaching the gift of fire."

"All over Dragor?"

"Oh far further than that," said Ketu. "Now we dragons stay in Dragor's boundaries for our safety. But before than we were scattered over the wide world beyond."

Yoshiko felt a little flash of excitement. He'd never known there was anything beyond Dragor.

"But the humans gave chase, and there was a great battle during which many many dragons were slain."

Ketu looked sad. "Then," he continued "the dragons were losing the battle at the foot of the mountain, and Surion was slain."

Yoshiko gasped.

"Goadah's heart was broken to see the death of his son," he said. "And he gave out such a cry that the mountain exploded in hot fiery liquid from the earth itself. It tumbled out and caused the humans to flee. Then the dragons escaped through a tunnel within the rock as the mountain fell behind them, sealing the pathway forever, and the dragons were afforded their protection. Dragor is protected by the volcano we now call 'Surion' in honour of his name, and the clans built The Fire Which Must Never Go Out to keep us from sight. Now the humans believe dragons are just a legend and we are safe. Some dragons still believe that the spirit of Surion lives on within the volcanoes which surround Dragor. When you hear them rumble it is his roar, and sometimes they make a great pounding sound like a heartbeat."

"Will the humans ever come back?" asked Yoshiko.

"No," said Ketu. "We are safe in Dragor. But we can never leave, according to the Commandments of Goadah. There is something else Yoshiko," he said. "Different clans tell the tale differently. Some like the Alana's still believe that Surion's egg was a curse to the dragons. That we were better off working for the humans, who provided us food."

"What about me?" asked Yoshiko suddenly. "Was

I born to a special egg like Surion? Is that why the Hudrah wanted to take me away?"

From across the cave Kiara's head popped up in alarm.

"No," she said quickly. "You must never say things like that. Not even as a joke."

Yoshiko's face twisted grumpily.

"Why don't you go and practise your fire making?" said Ketu, glancing at Kiara. "It's your first day at Fire School tomorrow." He followed sensing her desire to end the tales.

Since Yoshiko had been old enough to understand that flames came from the mouths of dragons he had been desperate to make his own fire. His attention switched instantly.

"I'm going to blow a big jet of flame!" Yoshiko announced, scuttling off towards where his flame target was kept.

Officially young dragons did not make flames until their official Fire Ceremony, in which they lit their first torch. But Kiara and Ketu's son practised daily.

Not that he had any success so far. Despite his father's patient coaching Yoshiko had not even managed a tiny puff of smoke.

"Come on then Yoshiko, let's set up the target," said Ketu, drawing his hatchling to the back of the cave. They retrieved the little diamond-shaped target from where it had been stored and raised it to be level with Yoshiko's snout.

Ketu had bought the target from the mountainous Talana territory, taking the advice of Guard Captain Ayo. "Believe me Ketu," Ayo had said. "I see elders buy the target for their first hatchling from the Nephan Market – but what sort of quality do you think you will get there? Metalwork from Nephans that's what, and we all know what that means."

All the dragons knew that blue Talanas were by far the most skilled clan when it came to making heavy metalwork. But social Nephans were far better at bringing useful goods to the market place, and a few less honest sorts were even known to pass off their substandard metal objects as Talana-made.

"You show me the Talana dragon who will willingly bring their own goods to market and I'll show you a dragon who is actually half Nephan" continued Ayo, repeating the popular theory that even the most talented of the Talanas were reclusive. "You take my advice Ketu," said Ayo. "I've seen more melted targets than you've drunk fresh sorrel juice. Go direct to the Talana Mountains and buy your hatchling a titanium target from there. It will last you twenty winters and cost you half what you'd pay in the market."

So Ketu had duly followed Ayo's instructions and headed to the jumble of dark mountains which made up the Talana territory. There he'd found a sturdy target for two glass-stones and returned with it to find Yoshiko beside himself with excitement.

A few months later and Ketu looked sadly at the

target which had not yet suffered a single blast of flame, save for the first practice shot he'd made as an example for his son. At this rate the durable metal would last him and Kiara five hatchlings and a great many more winters besides.

Yoshiko puffed up his chest, ever eager to give his all to the practice, and seemingly undeterred by his many previous failures.

"Think from your belly," advised Ketu, as Yoshiko made yet another attempt to light the family's hearth fire. "Breathe from your belly instead of your lungs, and click your tongue up like this" and he made a loud clicking sound, causing sparks to fly.

Yoshiko tried to copy and this time emitted a loud belch which caused Ketu to fall about laughing.

"You'll get it right soon," he encouraged. "We'll practise again tomorrow." And he patted Yoshiko on the head. "Plenty of time for fire games."

Kiara looked up from her wooden canvas at the father and son. But though she didn't say anything, she was worried. All the other dragons Yoshiko's age had begun to go through Metamorphism, where their bellies started to produce gases to make flame, and the bones in their mouths hardened to flint. But Yoshiko had given no sign that any physical changes were taking place.

Although dragons were naturally built to make fire they needed training to bring the gift to the surface, and most young Nephan dragons could make little puffs of smoke and flame. But even with Ketu's patient tuition Yoshiko had not produced so much as a spark.

She voiced her concerns to Ketu later as the family roosted on the roof their cave and Yoshiko's breathing came steadily from his perch in a thin whistle.

"His friends are all making fire," said Kiara. "And he has not come anywhere near even needing that target." Ketu drew his wing more tightly around her.

"Fleter has been training his daughter almost from birth to make fire," he said reassuringly. "And she still only makes little flames. The hatchlings are young still. It isn't like Yoshiko will be seven winters and unable to blow flames."

Kiara snuggled closer but she couldn't bring herself to say what she was most worried about. That the egg had heralded something about her son. Something different. So instead she said:

"There was all that silly trouble about his birth. I don't want him to be picked on if he is a late developer. Some of the dragons haven't forgotten and their hatchlings might think of him as different."

Since the birth it was an unspoken understanding that neither Ketu of Kiara would talk about the bright coloured egg shell, not even to Yoshiko.

"It is his first day at fire training tomorrow," said Ketu. "Many dragons don't blow any fire until they are trained by Ayo, but go on to be the best flame-throwers in Dragor." This at least was true and Ayo regularly remarked upon the fact that practice prior to coming to his Fire School made no difference to skill by the end of the ten years.

Kiara looked over to where Yoshiko was sleeping, his little red body barely discernable in the night. "Do you remember when he got scared of the dark and perched up here with us?" she said. The three of them had slept in Kiara's nest until Yoshiko's claws were strong enough to perch and then Ketu had made him his own little ledge, but he had often come to roost with his elders.

"Maybe we shouldn't have let him. Perhaps we should have encouraged him to stay on his own perch." said Kiara. But Ketu reassured her.

"All young dragons perch with their elders for a few nights. There is nothing unusual about that and I'm sure he will make fire when he is at Fire School like all the other dragons."

Kiara smiled and closed her eyes. But it was many hours before either of them slept.

"The little Nephan runt who
is not old enough for Fire School can
even make a better fire!" continued
Igorr, obviously trying to keep the
taunts in full force. "We shall have
to call you Feddy after the dragon
who couldn't make flames!"

Chapter Six

Fire School

Yoshiko was up and pestering his parents hours before school was due to start. And eventually it was a tired Ketu who dropped down from his perch to calm his excitable son.

"I can't eat morning food!" announced Yoshiko. "It will curdle in my stomach and I won't be able to make any fire." But Ketu had already drawn out the heavy pan and was filling it with salt-rock and herbs. He blew a little spurt of fire into the mixture and stirred in some dark peat.

"You'll need as much food inside you as you can get to give you all the energy to make flames," he announced, heaping a little wooden bowl and placing it on the stone table where the family ate their meals.

Yoshiko studied the mixture warily. Ketu was a good cook, but sometimes his inventiveness got the better of him and in a spirit of innovation he added strange ingredients to otherwise usual meals. He was also prone to dishing up meals which were too healthy for his son's liking.

Kiara flopped down from her perch and Yoshiko eyed her hopefully. "Can I please have treacle-fruit pancakes?" he asked, trying to keep his tone casual.

But Kiara had already seen the bowl of wholesome peat porridge.

"Not when your elder has already made your morning food," she said, helping herself to a ladle of sorrel juice from another cauldron. "Here," she added, handing him a wire net. "You'll need this for today."

Yoshiko took it happily. He'd seen other young dragons using the copper nets to carry their equipment to school and always envied the casual way in which they hooked them over their wings. The shape made it possible for the dragon to hold many items securely whilst in flight, and though Yoshiko would not start flying training for another few seasons the prospect of owning his own school net was an exciting one.

"It has your midday meal in it and the equipment that Ayo asked you to bring" explained Kiara.

She stuck her snout into the net and retrieved a heavy glass jar in her teeth.

"Put this on," she added, nudging the little pot towards him. "Make sure you cover your chest completely, and don't forget your ears."

Before their scales hardened younger dragons suffered in the intense heat of Fire School. So concerned elders smeared their hatchlings with the thick oily pressings of whale-fruit to protect them from painful scalds. Yoshiko opened the jar and recoiled at the smell.

Kiara snatched it up and began smearing it thickly

on his chest as Yoshiko wriggled and grimaced. "You won't mind the smell when you get scale-ache from the fire," she said. "Be sure to put it on again after you've eaten at midday."

But even the scent of the whale-fruit couldn't dim Yoshiko's mood as he hooked the wire school-net through his wing and climbed onto his father's back. Ketu took off gracefully as Kiara waved from the cave entrance and soon they were in a thick airborne stream of other elders taking their hatchlings for the first day at Fire School.

The dragons banked east, and Yoshiko looked curiously out from Ketu's back. "Why are we flying this way?" he asked. "It's quickest to fly west over the mountain."

"Well spotted Yoshiko," said Ketu. "If we flew that way we would all pass over Cattlewick Cave, and Guya is a dragon who likes to live quietly."

"What is Cattlewick Cave?" Yoshiko was intrigued.

"Cattlewick Cave is a great cave to the west of Nephan Clan," said Ketu. "Only Guya lives there, and dragons do not get close enough to risk bothering him."

"Who is Guya?" asked Yoshiko.

"No one really knows much about him," said Ketu. "But Guya is a Nephan dragon and some say he displeased Kinga."

"Our great leader?" said Yoshiko.

"Yes, but I don't know if it is true" said Ketu. "I do

know that Kinga is certainly a good and fair leader, and is much loved by the clans. Kinga ruled that Guya must be left alone and others think he must be doing some good for Dragor."

"He lives all by himself?" asked Yoshiko, trying to imagine how a dragon could live all alone.

"All by himself" repeated Ketu, wheeling back west towards the Fire School with the flock of other dragons.

Ayo was on his haunches with his wings wide in welcome as the dragons came to land, and Yoshiko couldn't stop staring at the dark red scales. They were thicker than any he had ever seen on a grown up dragon, and he wondered what possible weapon could pierce the armour.

"That's from all his years of training," said Ketu, following the direction of his son's gaze. "Ayo has trained with the Guard Dragon all his life, and is in the elite rank – The Fire Walkers."

Yoshiko looked on awestruck. He had heard of the Fire Walkers, but had never seen one in the flesh. They were the most highly regarded in the Guard Dragon, and were known for their daily rituals to strengthen their scales. They earned their name by a fearsome ability to stand the high temperatures in specially heated caves. All dragons who were elected as guards for Dragor underwent regular practice in fire pits, but The Fire Walkers trained for years and their scales were too thick to be pierced by any spear.

Ayo himself kept a pit of blazing white fire burning

near the entrance of his school for his daily training. The fire heated a great cave known as the Fire Pit, in which dragons braved the fierce heat to toughen their scales, and Ayo himself used it often toughening his scales to a deep dusty red. Yoshiko looked at his own skin, which was so soft that the scales were barely separated and then back to Ayo, whose body was covered in thickly raised ridges. He decided to train hard every day.

"When can the hatchlings walk into the Fire Pit?" he asked Ketu.

"Not for many seasons yet," said his father. "At first even standing at the entrance near the hot stone walls will give you scale-ache, but after the first week you won't need the whale-fruit, and after a few moons you'll be able to walk into the outside of the Pit. Then one day long in the future you might be good enough to walk right into the centre."

"Besides," he added. "You are only a hatchling for your first few seasons at Fire School. When you can fly and blow fire you will be a youngling like the other pupils."

"Then a warrior dragon?" Yoshiko's eyes were gleaming with the idea of his extra status.

"Not for a long time yet," said Ketu. "But one day yes we hope. And when you have hatchlings of your own you will be an elder like Kiara and I."

Yoshiko looked into the depths of the Fire Pit, which was glowing red hot.

Behind it stood the Fire School itself, and Yoshiko soaked up the image. To the front stood two large torches which acted to form an entrance to an enormous crescent. The sides were stacked high with rocks to prevent any fire escaping, and from the top of this tall wall was an observation deck from which other dragons could witness the spectacles below.

Already to the edge of the crescent numerous targets had been laid out, and fledgling dragons – those who had reached seven winters – were belching out mighty columns of flame, and striking up against the metal in a dizzying flash of light.

"Those are the trainee guards" explains Ketu. "Not every dragon makes Guard Dragon status, but those who do train every day to keep their fire strong and powerful." Yoshiko knew that Ketu had once been a Guard Dragon and still kept some of his former strength in his flames.

"Are those the dragons we see perched defending Dragor?" he asked in wonder. Guard Dragons usually kept far away from the other dragons, but their large bodies and tough scales could be seen on the tallest mountains. Yoshiko had only ever seen them from a distance before, and up close their thick skins and huge bodies were a little frightening.

"Yes but those are only in training," said Ketu. "The real guards are much bigger up close."

Behind the trainees was the largest cave Yoshiko had ever seen. It would take the entire Talana clan a hundred moons to carve out such a structure he thought. From his position near the entrance he could only see dark paths leading into the rock, but it was clear from how far back the cave progressed that it went very deep.

Outside the entrance was a mighty stone tablet, on which were etched the words THE COMMANDMENTS OF GOADAH. Like most hatchlings Yoshiko had been taught the commandments from birth, and knew very well the penalties of disobeying them. Although it was hardly ever used, Dragor had a prison of sorts. A dark thick cave that even a Talana couldn't tunnel its way out of and guarded by the fiercest of the Guard Dragons.

Yoshiko read through the commandments in his head.

1. NEVER LEAVE DRAGOR

He understood this to be the most important commandment of them all. No dragon must ever leave Dragor. To do so was to put all the dragon clans in danger of being discovered again by humankind, who would surely try to enslave them. After the mighty battle to save their species from man many dragons had died, and none wanted to relive the nightmare of that war.

2. NEVER FLY ABOVE SURION MOUNTAIN

The tallest mountain in Dragor stood directly facing Yoshiko's cave. It reminded him of the brave Surion every time he looked at it, and served as a marker above which no dragons were allowed to fly. By day and night The Fire Which Must Never Go Out and the mist from the mud pools threw up a tall smoke that helped to conceal Dragor from the rest of the world. But if a dragon flapped their wings above the height of Surion Mountain they might be seen by others.

3. ALWAYS KEEP ALIGHT 'THE FIRE WHICH MUST NEVER GO OUT'

Part of the Guard Dragon duty was to ensure the fire was kept aflame with its smoke to keep Dragor hidden, and it was one of the greatest honours to guard the fire. Though it was a weary business staying up overnight to fuel the flames, young dragons competed for it in Fire School, and no-one had ever fallen asleep on guard duty. Yoshiko wondered if he might ever be given the chance to prove himself, and sent up a little wish into the sky. Then he wrinkled his snout grumpily. So far he couldn't even make a little flame.

4. RESPECT THE ELDERS

Yoshiko nodded at this. He knew it was important to respect his elders, but he wondered how old Goadah had been when he made the commandments. Dragons could live to over one hundred and twenty years before their time came to fly to the burial ground, and older dragons commanded respect.

Ketu looked over Yoshiko's shoulder. "Reading up on Goadah's Commandments?" he commented, "Kiara will be pleased". Ketu often teased his partner that she only taught Yoshiko to read because she was so worried he wouldn't realise what the dragon laws were and get himself in trouble.

Not that any dragon who could read could avoid them. The Commandments were posted up in all the meeting places of the clans, as well as the market place and by The Fire Which Must Never Go Out.

Fleter landed beside them with his girl hatchling Amlie on his back and Ketu turned to greet his old friend. "Remember our first day at Fire School?" he asked, nudging Fleter jovially with his wing. "You nearly singed my tail!"

Amlie hopped down from his back, carrying an identical net to Yoshiko. They touched wings, and both broke into wide smiles. Amlie and Yoshiko lived in the caves nearest to one another, and as younger hatchlings regularly played in the Nephan mountains.

"I didn't think you would be coming to Fire School this year," said Yoshiko. Amlie was a particularly small dragon, and there had been some debate as to whether she should enter the school with dragons her own age.

"My elders knew I wanted to be in the same class as

you," she replied. "And so I practised and practised to make a flame. Look!"

She swelled her small chest to an impossible size, screwing up her face in the process and gasped out a rush of air that smelled like paraffin, but no fire accompanied it.

"Wait," she said, inflating herself again. This time the exhalation was met with a little shower of sparks, and the tiniest flame, no more than a talon-width across hung off her bottom lip.

Yoshiko was impressed.

"I can do better," said Amlie. "I always get the timing wrong. You have to match the air and the spark. But my elder says I'll soon be spurting long jets of flame."

A sudden sound drew everyone's attention. Ayo had blasted out an enormous fireball signalling it was time for school to begin.

"All the hatchlings into the main crescent!" he announced. "Elders who wish to stay and watch their hatchlings for the first day may assemble behind."

Amlie and Yoshiko exchanged glances, and with barely a backward look at their elders ran towards the entrance. Behind them Fleter and Ketu made their way more slowly to the observation deck.

As the hatchlings and elders divided a purple dragon landed with a loud thud. He was obviously far later than any of the other arrivals, but didn't seem in any rush. Instead he unfurled his large wing casually and let his purple Alana hatchling hop down. The father had a shifty look to his face and the little dragon had a look that seemed to suggest he already hated Fire School and everyone in it. He was large for his age with the hard scales of a hatchling who'd been left to play too close to the cave fire.

Ketu turned to Fleter. "Gandar is late as ever," he said. "Do you think he will stay to watch his son's first day?"

Fleter gave a little snort of amusement. "He'll be straight back in the sky and off to warm himself in the mud pools as soon as the little one enters the school."

The young purple dragon headed for the two torches which blazed to signal the entrance of the crescent. Inside all the small hatchlings were already lined up with Ayo standing in front of them.

"You must be Igorr," he said kindly as the new arrival sped through the door. "Take your place with the other hatchlings." And he pointed over to where Amlie and Yoshiko were huddled with their ears quivering in excitement. Amlie nodded at Igorr, but he only glowered back at her.

"My elders say I should mix only with Alanas," he said, looking around busily to where some other purple dragons were huddled. Amlie made a face at Yoshiko and he hid a smile. But before either of them could make a retort the attention of all the hatchlings was drawn back to Ayo as he beat his wings together causing the great torches to flare.

71

"Welcome to Fire School!" he announced. "All of you young hatchlings will learn to blow flame by the time you leave, and some of you will learn to blow flame very well." he paused. "The dragon's fire is our greatest accomplishment. It enabled us to win our freedom from humankind who would have enslaved us. But it can also be a curse." he waited as a ripple of surprise ran through the young hatchlings.

"The greatest strength can be the greatest weakness," he continued. "And although the flame is a mighty force what we teach here is respect for the power which has been granted to us by the great Surion."

"In Dragor the most talented dragons use their fire to great purpose. The Talanas make exquisite metalwork, the Efframs fire the most beautiful pots from the red clay of their hills," he waved his wings expansively. "But fire can also destroy, and you young hatchlings must leave as fine young dragons who know how to use your powers wisely."

Igorr was staring intently at the torches as Ayo spoke, and Yoshiko could see he was far more interested in making fire than learning the rules. He looked around to see Ketu and Fleter watching their hatchlings with interest, and then noticed the dark stare of a large Alana dragon. That must be Igorr's elder, thought Yoshiko, seeing Gandar for the first time.

Ayo was motioning for the hatchlings to follow him, and to their dismay they followed him not to the array

72

of gleaming targets, but inside the large cave.

"Are we not going to learn to use the targets?" asked Amlie, glancing anxiously back over her shoulder at the older dragons belching fire. "Why are we going inside?"

Yoshiko didn't know either, so he kept silent as they went into the school. The long dark tunnels seemed to wind on forever as they followed Ayo up into the far reaches of the school and eventually reached a large open cave where the roof had been cut away to allow some natural light to flow in. Little bays had been cut into the floor in a semi-circle shape, and one by one the hatchlings stretched out in them with Ayo in the centre.

He pulled down a heavy flat tablet of stone using a tough-looking system of cogs and then turned another lever to roll a thin panel of flat wood over its surface. Using thin streams of fire from his nostrils rather than his mouth he burned two words carefully into the blank wood.

"Fire Lessons"

Yoshiko and Amlie had been some of the last dragons to enter the room, and with only a few spaces left Igorr was once again forced to sit with Nephans rather than his own Alana clan. He looked at them both coldly as if they were somehow responsible.

"Don't blame us if you can't sit with Alanas," said Amlie, catching his expression. "You should have got here on time." Igorr glared at her.

"Take out your boards and your charcoal" instructed Ayo from the front, and all the hatchlings dug around in their nets to bring out the relevant equipment. As younger dragons they were not yet adept at making the delicate trails of fire needed to scorch words into wood or paper. This talent was made into an art form by the yellow Bushki clan, who used their dexterous snouts to make breathtakingly beautiful lettering on the documents and books they made for the other dragons.

For the hatchlings who couldn't breathe fire, charcoal sticks had been made to use on wooden boards. This meant the writing could easily be wiped away with a handful of sand and the board reused in class.

Yoshiko hadn't thought too deeply about why there was a charcoal and a board in his bag, and it occurred to him that Fire School might not be as exciting as he'd hoped. He glanced over to Igorr expecting him to look even crosser at the mention of writing rather than flame-throwing, but the purple dragon's muzzle was twisted in confusion and he was looking about him anxiously.

"Have you not brought anything with you?" said Amlie in a shocked voice. Igorr didn't seem to have a net of his own.

"How was I supposed to know?" grumbled Igorr, looking distraught as all the other pupils looked up with their wooden boards poised expectantly. "No-one told me I needed to bring... whatever that is" and he gestured uncertainly to the stick of charcoal.

"Here, you can share mine," said Yoshiko, moving the board between them. Igorr looked up with a reluctant gratitude, and then Ayo began to speak.

"You young hatchlings probably want to get straight out and start practising on those targets," he said. "But before you're allowed anywhere near the real thing you'll be taught dragon-anatomy, fire-sense, fire-theory and the history of Surion. When you've learned all these areas of tuition to the proper standard then we'll start teaching you to make fire properly with your snouts."

He stopped and pointed the edge of his wing meaningfully around the circle of hatchlings. "Until that time I don't want to see any of you making fire at Fire School. I know most of you have learned some skills at home and may even be able to hit a target. But until I say you make fire, no-one makes fire. Is that understood?"

Igorr looked proud when Ayo suggested some dragons could hit a fire target, but soon looked annoyed again. "What is the point of learning all this stuff if we can do it already?" he said to Yoshiko, clearly forgetting his previous desire to mix only with Alana clan dragons. "I can hit a target from twelve paces, so why do I need to know about this other stuff?"

Yoshiko, reminded of his own lack of fire skills,

wondered if the other dragon really could do so well already. Privately he was not sorry that all the hatchlings had to learn the theory first. He hoped that he'd be able to pick up the basics and catch up with his classmates who could make fire before anyone noticed he was behind.

"However," said Ayo, as if he'd overheard Igorr. "I know that many of you young hatchlings will have come here today very excited and perhaps all ready to make a flame or two. And many of you also have elders who have come to watch you on your first day at Fire School. So as a special treat for today only we will be doing a little target play just before midday. After that if I see any fire from you youngsters I will be contacting your elders to have them fly you home early."

He looked at them sternly, and seeing his point had been made continued with the lesson.

"This morning we learn about your bodies, and how they make fire," said Ayo. "What is the most important part of fire breathing?" he asked, staring around the room for an answer. A young Bushki dragon called out from the front row.

"The fire-gases!"

Ayo peered to where he was sitting. "Very good," he said. "That's an important part of making fire. And for those of you who don't know, there are fire gases being made in all your little bellies as we speak."

He looked out over the hatchlings. "When a dragon

enters his second winter the shape of his stomach begins to change," he explained. "It develops deep pits which create two different liquids. And when these are mixed together they blend into a special volatile gas that can be breathed out of the throat to make flame. Who can tell me what volatile means?"

Another Bushki dragon spoke out. "Flammable," she said. "It means you can set it on fire."

"That's correct," said Ayo. "And all of you have these pits in your stomach as we speak. That's why you'll have gone through a stage known as Metamorphosis. Do you remember? When your stomach started to make noises of its own accord and you developed an embarrassing tendency to burp in public?"

The hatchlings giggled. Most had gone through Metamorphosis with its commonly known side-effect a few seasons ago, but some were still suffering the last of its anti-social effects. As if in response to Ayo a small Talana dragon's stomach growled noisily and the hatchlings near where he sat roared in amusement.

Whilst they were laughing Ayo had sketched out a long ridged structure on the wooden school-board.

"What do you think this is?" he asked the nearest dragon, a blue Talana who blushed a shade bluer and lowered her little horn.

"I... don't know," she stuttered, looking around her to see if what she'd just declined to answer was obvious. But all the other hatchlings looked blank.

"You just used it," said Ayo. He was met with more blank stares. And then Yoshiko raised a tentative wing.

"It's a tongue," he said.

Ayo nodded. "Quite right. That's exactly what it is. You all have one in your mouths. And there's something very special about them. You might not have even realised it, you who can already make fire. But the dragon tongue is vital in making flames."

He clicked his own tongue and a few sparks shot forth.

"See these ridges here," he pointed to the drawing on the school-board. "The technical name for these is diamond-protrusions." Several pupils scribbled this down. "They are also known as carbon-teeth." he pointed to the shape of the ridges, which were curved slightly like tiny claws.

"These curved shapes are one half of what makes the sparks that ignite the flame," said Ayo. "And every dragon is born with these. Even tiny hatchlings have the little diamond-protrusions on their tongues," he paused. "But when a dragon is small they have not yet formed another important part of making fire." This time Ayo tapped the top of his mouth with a claw.

"The flint bones," he said, "harden around the top of the mouth. And when they are properly set the tongue can be used to strike against them and make sparks."

He drew a mouth around the tongue on the board and tapped at it. "The basic technique is very simple," he said. "But it does not usually come naturally, and is most often taught. Can anyone tell me a dragon for whom this method was a natural skill?"

Now all the hatchlings flung their wings up jostling to be chosen. Ayo pointed out an orange Mida dragon.

"Surion!" he announced proudly. "It was Surion who first taught fire to the other dragons!"

Ayo nodded. "That's right," he said. "Surion born of the red egg. He knew naturally how to make fire and taught the other dragons so that we might be freed from our slavery to the humans. But for most of us..."

He stopped to click his tongue again, and a further spray of sparks flew out and made little black marks on the boards of the hatchlings in the front row.

"The technique must be learned."

At the front of the class a wing went up. A dark blue Saigo dragon was trying to get Ayo's attention.

"What is it?" he asked.

"Is it true that Surion brought a curse on dragon-kind?" asked the dragon.

Ayo shook his head. "I am not going to get into the debate as to whether the coming of Surion brought dragon-kind freedom or cursed us to live in hiding," he said. "That is for your history class teacher. And I know how we different clans like to argue amongst ourselves about Surion. But there will be none of that here. In my classroom you'll all get along."

He turned to the board again, motioning towards the picture. "The basic method is that the very tip of the tongue must curl back to strike the very back of the jaw. We'll be learning in more detail throughout the season the different ways of doing this, and you'll also find out how different sparks can cause different types of fire. But for the beginning I imagine all of you will want to make the biggest flames you possibly can."

The hatchlings nodded enthusiastically.

"Well then," said Ayo. "Let's get outside and give you a practice." He unfolded his wings to gesture them to get up from their seats.

"When we come back in the afternoon you'll be far more interested in the technique," he added. "But for now I think it's time we let you at those targets before some of you combust."

And he led the troop of young dragons back out into the winding corridors of the cave.

As they trotted behind him the hatchlings passed other classes being taught fire skills and dragon laws. Yoshiko overheard a lesson on the history of Dragor floating past and wondered when it was they would find out more details about their homeland.

Eventually the dark cave opened out into the wide crescent where they'd first come in, and to Yoshiko's surprise the elder dragons were still clustered into the viewing deck above them. He waved at Ketu who raised his wing in reply.

Igorr, who had been sour-faced since starting the school suddenly began to smirk and look happy.

"There is my elder!" he cried, grabbing Yoshiko in his excitement. "Do you see him? He has come to watch me make fire." he started waving frantically.

Yoshiko looked up into the viewing deck to see a purple dragon with hooded eyes staring down at them. The older Alana nodded his snout slightly, but didn't return his son's wave. Then he looked up at the sun, as if calculating how much longer he would need to spend at the school.

"Line up in front of the targets!" Ayo was arranging the hatchlings in neat rows. "Today you'll stand at the practice line," he said, moving them forwards to a deep line that had been etched into the ground before the targets. "This might seem a long way from the targets to you now, but in three winters you'll be firing at them from right over there." he pointed to the far back of the crescent where several numbered lines were drawn in the floor. These must be the proper test stands, realised Yoshiko, whilst where they stood was for little hatchlings only and was not even graded by number. He looked back to the lines in the distance, and wondered whether he would ever be able to throw fire that far.

"Now," said Ayo. "I know that many of you can already make some little flames. And I know some of you may not yet have grasped it, or have not practised at all and would rather sit this attempt out and wait until you can give the targets a proper blast. So anyone who would like to give their go a miss please wait at the side here and watch how the other hatchlings try."

Around half a dozen began to shuffle over to the edge of the crescent and several of them looked very relieved.

Yoshiko watched them uncertainly, and then looked back to Amlie who was almost bursting with impatience to start. He would try it out, he thought, even though he risked looking stupid. Maybe something about the proper targets at the Fire School would unleash some hidden potential which hadn't yet come out.

Trying to keep himself from showing his concerns, he stepped in beside Amlie's line. Looking up at the viewing deck he noticed that Ketu looked proud of his choice, and his worries grew a little smaller. "Better to try and fail than never try," he muttered to himself, repeating one of Kiara's favourite mottos.

Igorr had finally found himself some fellow Alanas to fall in with, and was puffing out his chest, clearly confident at his talent in making fire. Yoshiko tried to copy the gesture, pulling in his belly in the hope it would make the fire gases more effective.

At Ayo's command the dragons at the front of the rows started the practice. Around half managed to command a full flame that left their bodies, whilst the others made only sparks, or little jets of fire which didn't really leave their mouths. No-one hit a target.

"Next!" called Ayo, and the first dragons shuffled

away to join those watching in the wings whilst the second group took their place. This time, without the pressure of being first, the dragons seemed to perform even better. And as the line of waiting dragons got smaller some almost hit the target. It was obvious that the Efframs were the most naturally gifted with fire, as time and time again the green hatchlings made the best attempts. But all the young dragons were trying their hardest.

In front of Yoshiko Amlie moved forward to her place in front of the target. And under Ayo's command she puffed up her chest and unleashed a football-sized flame that fell within a few feet of the target.

She turned to Yoshiko delighted. "Did you see that?"

He smiled at her, and she turned her snout up to the viewing deck where Fleter was on his feet waving and shouting. Amlie gave a proud smile and walked away to the edge of the group.

Yoshiko was nervous suddenly. He turned to the blue Talana dragon behind him, who had been jiggling impatiently to get near the target.

"Would you like to go in front?" asked Yoshiko. He wanted just a few more minutes to prepare himself. The Talana dragon nodded gratefully and moved ahead, giving him a smile.

Yoshiko looked carefully down the line as the hatchlings prepared to take aim. Igorr had stepped up, he noticed, and was eyeing the target with an assured look. He balled up his chest, narrowed his eyes, and as Ayo gave the word let out an impressive column of flame which came close enough to nudge the edge of his target.

Ayo beat his wings in applause, and Igorr looked overjoyed, and turned to the viewing deck to see his elder's reaction. But the happiness dropped suddenly from him, and his wings collapsed despondently against his body.

Yoshiko turned to see that Igorr's elder was no longer watching from the viewing deck. He must have already left, and had not seen his son's fire at all.

Igorr stalked past the row of hatchlings, and as he did Yoshiko put out a friendly wing. "Why is your elder not here?" he asked, and Igorr turned on him furiously.

"Why is my elder not here?" he spat. "Why should anyone's elder be here? I'm not a baby like you. I don't need my elder looking on." And he marched off to join the others, but as he joined the group he turned his full attention back to glare at Yoshiko.

Feeling even more disconcerted by the angry gaze, Yoshiko stepped forward to the mark, and on Ayo's command he puffed up his chest as Ketu had shown him. Keeping the target in sight he raised his tongue to the back of his mouth, and as the command came whoosh! He let out a stream of air from his belly, and clicked his tongue as fast as he could.

Nothing came out.

Yoshiko dropped his snout in embarrassment and a

cry came suddenly from the sidelines.

"Look at the Nephan hatchling! He comes forward
to hit the target and cannot even make a spark!"

He looked to the side to see the jibe had come from
Igorr, who was looking jubilant now and was nudging
his fellow Alanas to enjoy the joke. Yoshiko bowed his
head and walked back into the sidelines, not even
looking up to see if Ketu was watching.

"What is the point of having your elder here if you
can't even make a flame for him Nephan?" said Igorr
as Yoshiko passed him to join the group. "What a waste
of time it's been for him."

Amlie came and stood by her friend without saying
anything.

"The little Nephan runt who is not old enough for
Fire School can even make a better fire!" continued
Igorr, obviously trying to keep the taunts in full force.
"We shall have to call you Feddy after the dragon who
couldn't make flames!"

Feddy was a story-tale dragon who was born
unable to make fire, and was instead appointed
the job of running the market-place where flames
weren't needed. It was a popular story amongst young
dragons, but none of them wanted to be like Feddy.

Yoshiko felt his scales turning darker in his
embarrassment.

"Other hatchlings can't make fire," said Amlie, her
voice rising in anger. "At least Yoshiko was brave

enough to try!"

But Igorr turned his head as if he couldn't hear her.

"His name is Feddy from now on," he was saying to the other Alanas. And there was something so nasty in his look that they nodded in agreement rather than contradict him.

The rest of the day was spoiled for Yoshiko though he did his best to ignore the taunts from Igorr and the Alana dragons. But by the afternoon when they'd eaten their midday meal all the Alanas were calling him this, and the nickname had stuck.

By the time they trooped into the final class of the day Yoshiko had become disheartened. His first day at Fire School and already he seemed to have made an entire gang of enemies.

The History of Dragor was taught by a plump female dragon who had stayed out of the sun so long that her red Nephan scales had turned a dusty pink.

"I bet she never does any fire walking" whispered Amlie as they trooped into the cave. Yoshiko smiled in reply, a little lifted by the thought of the lesson ahead. The History of Dragor had always appealed to him. Igorr, however, who now seemed to have attached himself to a group of mean-looking Alana dragons, groaned loudly as they came into the class. Unlike the earlier room this one was laid out with small stone desks to allow the dragons to write more easily.

"Who wants to learn about history?" he said loudly.

"We already know how to make fire."

"Not all of us," said one of his friends, an Alana by the name of Bitt. "Weedy Feddy over there is probably desperate to learn about it." Igorr looked delighted at the joke and turned to check that Yoshiko had overheard.

"Take your places" called the teacher, the folds of her soft skin rippling as she spoke. She wrinkled up her eyes to peer at the board, and using a stick of charcoal started to write on the board.

"She can't use fire" whispered Igorr, and the two Alanas sniggered. The teacher whirled around, her tail catching the stone desk.

"I can still hear very acutely, however," she said, glaring at Igorr. "What is your name young hatchling?"

Igorr looked down at the floor, embarrassed, and muttered his name.

"Igorr?" said the teacher. "Well perhaps for this class you will learn to be less concerned with making fire, and more interested in how we dragons came to make it."

She dismissed him with another wave of her tail and Igorr sat down next to his fellow Alanas looking miserable.

"Look!" said Amlie as they took their places. "Your elder's name!" The desks had been scratched with all kinds of graffiti over the years and Yoshiko saw KETU etched into the stone.

"My name is Ma'am Sancy," said the teacher, raising

her voice to be heard over the class.

"In this class we will learn, not only about the history of Dragor, but further back still, to the legends of all the clans. We will learn about one another," she added loudly, to stress the importance of this point. "And maybe you little hatchlings will find out you are not so different across the clans after all."

Igorr snorted as if he thought this unlikely and then dropped his head again as Ma'am Sancy turned to stare at him.

"I hope I won't have any trouble with you young Alanas," she said, waving her charcoal stick towards them. "Or I will have to make you sit apart. But I shouldn't have thought you would want to miss this lesson. Because the first thing we learn about is your own clan."

Even Igorr looked a bit more interested at this.

"Who knows the story of how the Alanas came into the world?" she asked.

Yoshiko looked over at Igorr expecting him to be keen to relay the story, but to his surprise the purple dragon had ducked his head again and was looking furtively at the graffiti on his desk. Every Nephan dragon was told the tale of how their clan was made as a bedtime story, and Yoshiko had assumed it was the same all across Dragor. He thought back to the shifty-looking Gandar who hadn't bothered to stay to watch his son's first flame at Fire School. He certainly didn't look like the kind of elder who told stories.

Ma'am Sancy didn't seem to mind the silence. Instead she settled back onto her scales and began to tell the story in a low soothing voice.

"Long long ago, before Dragor existed," she began. "The clans were scattered in the different corners of the world. And the Alanas came from a cold and mountainous place. Dusted with snow most of the year round, and beautiful to be sure. But veiled only with the thinnest of green grass, and topped with sky the colour of ice."

She looked around the room to see the young hatchlings listening quietly. Ma'am Sancy had a special sort of voice, thought Yoshiko, which made everyone want to pay attention.

"Before the Alanas came the land was empty," said the teacher. "Nothing lived there but a great spirit who was very lonely. She was so sad that she lifted herself into the sky, and became the first great wind, blowing all over the land in search of some comfort."

"Stronger and stronger she grew, stretching herself across the earth, and forming a powerful spout of air which swept across the mountains and down into the sea. When she reached the ocean she began stirring the elements of earth and water like peat porridge in a pot." Ma'am Sancy's hands began to turn as if she was stirring porridge, and the hatchlings watched her transfixed.

"Round and round they went, churning and turning, until eventually from the sea was churned the first

Alana dragon. Just as butter is churned from milk the dragons were made flesh from the water, and that is why the Alanas are fisherfolk, and understand the lakes and the seas. Because truly they are of the water."

The Alanas in the room were looking proud.

"The great spirit was proud of her creations as she set them forth. And she knew they would be entertainment for her and cast away her loneliness. But she also knew there was nothing for the Alana dragons to eat" continued the teacher. "And unlike the land of the Efframs which is all of green and plenty, or the milk and honey place where the Talanas come from, there was nothing in the land to make food. So the spirit stirred the waters again, and silver fish leapt about from the depths. Then she took the noses of the Alanas she had made and squeezed them in the middle."

Ma'am Sancy made a pinching motion with her claws, and the dragons from the other clans all looked towards to Alanas to see their snouts were indeed thinner in the middle, as if squeezed by a giant hand.

"For those who haven't seen the Alanas fish, you should know they are perfectly made for the task," said Ma'am Sancy. The great spirit made them with thin long snouts to root out the fish and pull them from the Great Waters, and sharp claws to best catch hold of them. And if you have a competition to hold your breath with an Alana you'd better watch out! They have lungs inside those little chests and can go without air for longer than any other dragon."

Igorr looked smug and Amlie rolled her eyes. "I bet they don't know the story of the Nephans," she whispered. But Ma'am Sancy was moving around the dragons handing out books.

"Turn to page three," she commanded. "And work quietly answering the questions there." Yoshiko snuck a look at Igorr. At least it seemed as though someone had taught him to read, even though he'd managed to get sent off to Fire School without his net and didn't seem to know anything about his own clan.

The rest of the day went by in a whirl of teachings. They learned about the lovely green land where the artistic Effram clan had come from, and how the dragons had been shaped from the clay of the earth. This explained how they were so clever at using the red clay found in their own hills of Dragor to make pots and other stoneware for the dragons.

They were told they would have to learn to recite Goadah's Commandments off by heart if they couldn't already, and as they left the school the hatchlings trooped past the entrance to the school warily looking at the stone tablet of commandments. Igorr in particular looked very worried.

Ketu was waiting to fly Yoshiko home, and he noticed his son's despondent face as he climbed aboard his back. Next to him Fleter was busy finding out from an excited Amlie all about her event blowing fire. He smiled at Ketu and Yoshiko and then pumped his wings into flight.

Sensing Yoshiko's sadness, Ketu held back from joining his friend in the sky, and instead turned his head to face his son.

"I saw you today at the targets," he said. "I thought you were magnificent for going up there."

Yoshiko shook his head angrily. "They all laughed at me," he said. "I should have stayed with the babies who couldn't make fire."

Ketu settled back on his haunches. "I remember going to my first day at Fire School," he said. "And some dragons said that those who couldn't make fire already shouldn't be at Fire School. But you know what?"

Yoshiko shook his head.

"I bet those dragons who teased those who were less able with fire didn't do so well in the other classes," said Ketu. "And no-one teased them for that. Doesn't seem very fair does it? But I know why it happens."

Yoshiko looked intrigued.

"Why?" he asked.

"Because those dragons who aren't so good at the other classes are so ashamed they don't want anyone noticing," he said. "And they'd rather take attention off the important things that they can't do and pretend the most vital aspect of Fire School is the thing they can do well."

Yoshiko looked unconvinced. "It's called Fire School," he said. "Why is it called that if making fire isn't the most important thing?"

Ketu looked at his son. "Yoshiko, look around Dragor. How many dragons spend their days making fire?"

Yoshiko thought about this. "The Bushki clan do," he said uncertainly. "When they make books and papers. And the Talanas use it to make explosions when they build caves. And the Guard Dragons." He puffed up his chest as he said this, thinking of the fearsome looking guards who protected Dragor.

His elder shook his head gently. "The Bushkis only use fire for some of their most elaborate paperwork," he said. "Most of the time they use charcoal. Their main skill is in letters. Not in fire. And the Talanas spend most of their time digging with their horns. If they couldn't make fire it would take them longer, but they could still make beautiful caves."

Yoshiko frowned. "But you used to be a guard. And they use fire most of all."

"The guards are trained so they don't have to use fire," said Ketu. "And the best guards will never have to use it." He looked as if he was about to say something else and then he stopped himself, opening out his big wings.

"Ready to go?"

Yoshiko nodded and was silent for a few minutes as they took flight.

"I just wanted you to see me make fire," he said finally, with a sigh.

Ketu smiled. "I am prouder that you stood up there

and tried when you didn't think you could do it Yoshiko. Such a thing shows more character than the finest flame. You'll learn in time, and when you do you'll have a better understanding of the art because of what you went through to learn it."

For the first time since the target practice Yoshiko allowed himself to make a tiny smile in return. "I'm going to practise harder than any other dragon," he said.

"Something about the warmth of the
feeling seemed to grow inside
him, and he tried to catch hold of it
as he stared at the target. A picture
of fire was in front of him suddenly,
and he felt his scales tingle all over
in a strange rush."

Chapter Seven

Home Sweet Home

Kiara had made a limestone pie and was taking it from the embers of the fire when father and son returned home. After the flight Yoshiko had returned almost to his cheerful self, and he bounded into the cave sniffing at the delicious wafts of cooking smells.

"When can we eat it?" he said, giving Kiara a nuzzle.

"Give me a moment to get it ready," she said. "Why don't you go and practise on your target and I'll call you when we can eat."

Ever excited by the prospect of his shiny target Yoshiko trotted off obediently, and began sucking in air noisily as Ketu came to help Kiara ease the pie from the coals.

"Did he do alright today in school?" asked Kiara, anxious.

Ketu nodded. "You would have been very proud of him," he said. "He joined the practice ranks when other dragons who couldn't make fire sat it out. And he tried even though he couldn't do it, and some dragons laughed at him."

Kiara's face dropped.

"Other dragons laughed at him?"

But Ketu patted her reassuringly. "The important

97

thing is that he had the strength of character to get up and try. With that kind of bravery a few sniggers won't bother him. He'll learn to make fire, you'll see."

But Kiara looked far from convinced. "Who were the dragons who were laughing?" she said angrily.

"Who do you think?" said Ketu. "Gandar and Agna's hatchling was at the worst of it. He can already make good fire. But I imagine he's learned that from his elder at the expense of more important lessons."

Kiara scoffed. "He'll end up full of himself for his fire-making and thrown out of the Fire Guards, just like his elder."

Ketu raised a talon as a caution for her to keep her voice down. "No-one is supposed to know why Gandar was asked to leave the Fire Guard Kiara. If Yoshiko finds out it could be all over the school. And that would hardly be fair on Igorr would it? Besides, we don't want to be rumour spreaders. Leave that to the Alanas."

His mate lowered her head in response, but she still looked angry.

"I'll call Yoshiko in to help with the dinner" added Ketu, but Kiara touched his wing to stop him.

"No, no," she said. "Not if he's had a hard day at school. I'd rather he rest and enjoy himself at home."

From the other side of the cave Yoshiko could barely hear his elders, but he sensed something in their tone was wrong. Probably worried about their son's lack of ability to make fire, he thought grimly. Out of all the hatchlings who couldn't do it none had been a Nephan. Second to the Efframs they were known to be the best fire-makers, and it had been mostly Midas and Saiga clan dragons who had not gone up to try their luck on the targets.

A low feeling seemed to boil inside him. It wasn't fair! He had tried so hard. What if he was different from the other dragons? And then he remembered Ketu's voice on the flight home, telling him his elders were most proud of him because he tried, not because of what he achieved.

Something about the warmth of the feeling seemed to grow inside him, and he tried to catch hold of it as he stared at the target. A picture of fire was in front of him suddenly, and he felt his scales tingle all over in a strange rush.

Uncertain as to what to do Yoshiko drew in a deep breath and turned towards the target, with the sensations moving over his skin. And then to his great surprise, something strange happened. It was as though there was a voice inside him telling him what to do. He was breathing from a different, deeper place – not his stomach quite – but somewhere else. And from the back of his throat came a fizzing sensation, like electricity.

In a sudden burst a modest jet of flame flew out, falling short of the target, but coming halfway towards it.

Yoshiko's mouth dropped down in amazement. He

had done it! He had made the fire! And then he looked down at his belly.

To his shock it was no longer the rich red of the Nephan clan. It was orange. Like a flame.

He gasped, looking to find his arms and legs the same colour. Even his little claws throbbed with the new colour. He was literally glowing with it.

Then, almost as quickly as he'd noticed it the colour faded, and his body returned to the Nephan red. Yoshiko blinked, wondering if he'd imagined it. Cautiously he held out his claws, but they were undoubtedly back to their deep natural shade. It must have been a trick of the light, he decided, maybe something the target did by itself when the flame hit it. And immediately forgetting about the colour change he raced to where Ketu and Kiara were silently preparing the meal.

"I did it!" he shouted tugging at Ketu's wing and grabbing Kiara's by the claw. "I made fire!" he pointed back towards the target. "Come and see! I can do it!"

"Calm down Yoshiko!" laughed Ketu. "They'll hear you in the Bushki clan with all that shouting. Let's go and see then what you can do." And he let a delighted Yoshiko drag him towards the target as Kiara followed them smiling a little.

"See. Watch this" commanded Yoshiko, puffing up his chest. He tried to command the same feeling as before. The rich warmth in his belly and the sharp crackle in his mouth. And as they watched he blew out with all his might, and snapped a spark from his tongue.

"Well done Yoshiko!" said Ketu. No fire had emerged, but it was the first time his son had made a spark in front of another dragon. "You're nearly there," he said.

But Yoshiko was bolstered by his earlier achievement and determined not to give up. "Wait wait!" he said, catching hold of Ketu's wing. "I can do it. Really I can." And he puffed out his chest for another attempt.

This time as he blasted the air forward the spark caught and a tiny but perfect fireball spat forth. Ketu's eyes widened and Kiara clapped her wings together happily. Yoshiko danced around in glee.

"You see! You see!" he said. "It was much better before. A really big ball." He spread his claws wide to demonstrate.

"You'll always make the biggest fire when there's no-one around to see it at first," said Ketu. "But if you keep practising you'll soon be making fireballs every time."

"Can I miss the meal and keep practising?" asked Yoshiko, determined to show them a proper flame before bedtime.

"Not tonight Yoshiko," said Kiara. "Come and eat your limestone pie. You'll need all your energy for school tomorrow. At the memory of Fire School and Igorr the little dragon's face dropped a little.

"His wings beat without him thinking about it, and in a moment he was cresting up into the air. It almost felt too easy. Yoshiko flapped again, and the motion sent him spiralling up far higher than Igorr had done."

Chapter Eight

Flying High

"Come on Yoshiko!" Ketu huffed out impatiently. "Time to launch you off the flying rock!"

Yoshiko came out warily, the remains of his peat porridge still on his muzzle. He had filled out, his father noticed, during his first few months of Fire School, and he silently made a pact to tell Kiara to stop feeding their son so much sticky mash and dragon puffs. Yoshiko loved the sweet puffs, which the Saigo dragons plucked from low bushes in their clan lands and toasted until crunchy and warm over the fires. When he'd had a particularly hard time with Igorr's taunts he liked nothing better than coming back to the cave and eating handfuls of the sweet puffs, but the effect on his stomach had started to show.

Yoshiko had generally settled in at Fire School, but he had managed to make a firm enemy of Igorr, who took every opportunity to bully and tease him. The nickname 'Feddy' had stuck, and even some of the dragons who liked him tended to call him by the name without thinking. It had made Yoshiko more withdrawn than the other dragons, and his elders couldn't help but notice that the lively and loud young hatchling who'd started school a season ago was now silent and watchful. Even Amlie noticed, though she didn't seem to mind, and the pair went into their classes together that Autumn wing to wing.

But although Yoshiko was undoubtedly popular with many of his fellow hatchlings for his kind and gentle nature, Kiara couldn't help but worry. And in trying to make up for what she thought was going wrong at school she permitted the sweet-toothed Yoshiko rather more treats than he should strictly have been allowed, and let him off helping out in their family cave.

The result was the exact opposite to what she could have hoped. Plumped out by the extra portions of sweet mash her son was even slower than he had been before at the physical activities in Fire School, which only gave Igorr and his friends even more reason to laugh at him. And in letting him off chores she gave him the feeling that he couldn't do anything on his own. At least she didn't need to worry about his marks at school. When it came to Dragor's history he was top of the class.

"Let's get you on board then," said Ketu, ignoring his son's downcast face and gesturing to his back. "By the time we get back you won't need me to take you anywhere."

Yoshiko sighed in response. He was tired at being the worst at everything. And he thought that flying would be no exception.

"I'm taking you to our own special rock," said Ketu,

by way of encouragement. "No one will be there but you and me. You can practise all you want and no-one is going to see."

His son climbed aboard, and with a wave from Kiara they were soon airborne, floating through the mists of Dragor. Ketu gave an expert sweep of his wing and brought them to bear east, taking them out past the dragon's Burial Ground to a remote spot. Seeing the faded Seventh Moon tributes left by hopeful dragons to welcome the dead back to life Yoshiko began to take more interest. He leaned forward towards Ketu's ear.

"Where are we going?" he asked in wonder as the sweep of the graveyard fell away beneath them. "Are we going outside Dragor?"

Ketu shook his head sternly. "No dragon must ever leave Dragor Yoshiko. You know that. It is one of the uppermost rules of Goadah."

Yoshiko sat back, unwilling to be disappointed. He had secretly hoped that when he was older it would be discovered that brave older dragons such as his elders left Dragor all the time and experienced the world beyond.

They cruised closer to a large rock, under which a river ran, and Ketu settled to land, folding under his huge wings. Yoshiko hopped off his back and gazed in awe over the precipice. The waters beneath them looked calm and still. But it was a long way down.

"Is this where we try flying?" he asked.

Ketu nodded. "This is where my elder brought me to practise and his elder before him. Many dragons have special family spots around Dragor which are honoured by other clans, and only they use."

But as he spoke a sudden gust of wind made them both look up, and to Ketu's obvious annoyance Gandar landed heavily beside them both, with Igorr staring smugly from his back.

"I see you're in my son's flying practice spot," said Gandar, eyeing Yoshiko in obvious amusement. "And you've brought a hatchling not yet ready to fly."

Ketu replied calmly, though Yoshiko noticed a vein in his neck was throbbing. "This is my family's flying spot," he said. "Though you are welcome to share it."

Gandar shook his head haughtily. "My Igorr is a fine hatchling who I hear already far excels your son at fire making. He shall be a far better flyer, and I see no reason why he should have to waste time watching this little dragon," he made a scornful motion with his wing. "He will fall in the water all day," said Gandar. "If he learns to fly at all."

Ketu's eyes flashed fire, and for the first time Yoshiko realised what a formidable guard he must have been. But Gandar raised himself even higher on his haunches, clearly enjoying the effect he was having on the other dragon.

"You Nephan clan dragons think you have a right to everything because you are leaders," he continued.

"But there is nothing in history that says the red dragons are better at taking charge of the clans. Every dragon knows the Alanas have the greatest stamina and are the best protectors of Dragor. It should be us who make the decisions."

Ketu looked tired, as if it wasn't the first time he had heard such an argument. This strain of bitterness was well known in Dragor. Many Alanas felt that Nephans had ruled for too long, and that their own kind should have a chance as leaders, rather than simply acting as catchers of fish. The other clans, however, knew that the rebellious Alanas would cause as many problems as they solved if given the task of ruling, and voted for Nephans at every clan gathering.

"Where our sons learn to fly has nothing to do with Nephan leadership or anything else," said Ketu. "You know that this is our family flying place, and we landed before you did. But since the clans must work together in Dragor I am happy to share the rock."

He didn't look happy, however.

Igorr hopped down from Gandar's back looking not the least bit embarrassed at the scene. "We can practise over here," he said, pointing to an area on the other side of the rock. "Away from Feddy." His elder nodded. "As you wish Igorr." And they moved over to the far side.

Ketu looked at Yoshiko in surprise, but the younger dragon only shrugged. "It's what they all call me at school," he said, trying to sound as if he didn't care. But the look on his elder's face pained him enough that tears rose up. He didn't want Ketu to know that his son was humiliated by the other dragons. Yoshiko turned away, pretending to watch Igorr and Gandar. But there was a strange feeling in his stomach. It reminded him of the time he'd first blown fire. This time it was different. It wasn't a warm glow he felt, but something thick and dark. They had got to the rock first and now Igorr would watch his first attempts to fly, and no doubt report back on his inadequacies to the other hatchlings at school.

He took a deep breath and tried to shake the feeling away, but it stayed rooted inside of him.

"If you want me to go and say something to your teacher I can do," said Ketu, not fooled by the pretence. Yoshiko shook his head vigorously keeping his snout down.

"Usually it's better to report these things," continued Ketu. "If they're making you unhappy elders can help." He leaned closer. "Usually dragons who aren't nice to other dragons don't have any real friends themselves," he said. "They pick on others because it's the only reaction they can get. Not like you and your friends."

Ketu straightened up, sensing that Yoshiko wanted to change the subject, and turned the conversation to flying.

"See the river below?" he asked, pointing down

with his wing. "This keeps you safe Yoshiko. It looks like a long way down, but you'll need long enough to get plenty of air under your wings for the first few attempts."

He noticed his son looked anxiously down. "It looks further down than it is," he repeated. "You're better off having the distance."

Yoshiko looked over to Igorr and saw the purple dragon was staring at him mockingly. And then he turned and dropped like a stone over the edge of the rock. Then the beating of air could be heard and Igorr crested up triumphantly into the sky. He flapped low over the rock for a moment, and then sunk exhausted back to Gandar's side.

"Did you see!" crowed Gandar. "See that Ketu! Yoshiko will never fly as well as Igorr." he turned back to his son. "Show them again," he said. "Take another flight."

Igorr looked scared for a moment. "My wings hurt," he said. "I don't know if I can make it a second time." But Gandar glowered at him. "Do it again Igorr," he said. "Do not complain of tiredness. That is for weak little Nephans." And he pushed Igorr back towards the edge. The look of triumph had gone from his son's face, and instead the little dragon looked thoroughly drained. But he spread his wings again and threw himself from the edge.

This time there was a much longer pause before he rose again, and when finally Igorr's purple wings drew him above the rock his face had lost its strong purple colour. He barely managed to crest the edge of the rock, dropping uncertainly in the sky before throwing a single wing onto the ledge and bodily pulling himself over.

Gandar's expression was stony as his son righted himself, panting in exhaustion, and he turned away from him in disgust. "You are useless," he hissed. "You are not trying Igorr. I could do much better at your age."

The feeling that Yoshiko had been fighting down grew suddenly to a terrible peak. He didn't like Igorr, but couldn't help his heart aching for the young dragon, whose elder seemed unimpressed by such great efforts.

Without thinking he unfurled his own wings and charged towards the end of the rock, thinking only that he no longer wanted to witness Igorr's face wrinkled in distress. Ketu moved to stop him, but before he could Yoshiko had already flung himself away into the empty air.

He dropped sharply, feeling the rush of cool water racing up to meet him, and then something incredible happened. His wings beat without him thinking about it, and in a moment he was cresting up into the air. It almost felt too easy. Yoshiko flapped again, and the motion sent him spiralling up far higher than Igorr had done.

Feeling free and joyous he let the natural shape of his body lean against the sky, with the breeze billowing beneath him, and coasted on the air as he'd watched Ketu do so many times before. Then he turned smoothly and made a large circle over the rock.

Yoshiko took a quick look below, expecting to see Ketu looking up proudly at him, but to his surprise all the figures on the rock were staring in horror. Disconcerted he brought his wings inwards, wheeling unsteadily down, and landing in a clumsy tumble on the floor.

Ketu ran towards him and caught him up in his wings.

"Yoshiko, what's wrong?" he asked, staring into his son's snout. "What's happened to your scales?"

Yoshiko shook his head in confusion, seeing that both Igorr and Gandar were also looking on at him in alarm.

"What is wrong with your hatchling Ketu?" asked Gandar, sounding frightened. "He has turned Alana."

And to Yoshiko's horror he looked down to see that it had happened again. He had changed colour. But this time he was glowing purple, from head to toe.

"I expect what you saw was the reflection of the fire itself on your scales. And the second occasion, well, you were by a river which may have reflected the light back onto you."

Chapter Nine

The Herb Doctor

"I don't care that he has turned back to the right colour again" stormed Kiara, when Ketu told her the events of the day. "I am taking him to the doctor. No arguments." And rather than risk a battle with his anxious mate, Ketu conceded that Yoshiko should be taken to a herb doctor in the Saiga clan.

The Saigas were the herb growers and doctors who worked to keep Dragor well. It was a fact that dragons were becoming more and more of a sickly species, and caring for their health seemed an endless task. Before the Battle of Surion it was thought that dragon-kind were never afflicted with much illness, but in Dragor all of the clans increasingly had different problems which caused them suffering.

The book-loving Bushkis suffered from stomach pain and ulcers, and the mining Talanas found they kept getting ear infections and throat problems. The nature-loving Mida clan often had heartburn and fertility issues, and the hips and legs were causing the Nephans difficulties as well as many complaints of mental stress. Many dragons were taking prescribed herbs to try to help them.

The herb doctor's cave was always filled with dragon patients in all the different colours, but somehow Yoshiko wondered if the doctor had ever seen anything like what had happened to him.

"Yoshiko is it?" The doctor's voice was gruff and to the point. "Come and sit up on the table here and let's have a look at you."

"What seems to be the problem?" he added, looking at Kiara who was fretting over his well-being.

Her gaze moved to the doctor. "We're not sure," she said finally. "But my son seems to be changing colour. When he learned to fly he changed from red to purple, and he told us that before then, when he first blew fire, a similar thing happened. But that time thought he turned orange."

"I see." The doctor took out a long crystal and tapped it against Yoshiko's chest, listening intently. He nodded, made some notes and then drew out the hatchling's wings as wide as they could go. "Take a deep breath," he said. "And again."

Yoshiko obeyed, letting his wings rise and fall.

The doctor dropped them back down again, and pulled out a small torch from his desk and lit it with a little puff of fire. He shone the light into Yoshiko's eyes and ears. Finally he had him step onto a set of scales, and wrote down some numbers.

"I think I have the problem," he said finally, settling back down onto his haunches. Kiara looked anxious. "What is it?" she asked.

"There is nothing medically wrong with your son," said the doctor, and Kiara gave a great sigh of relief.

"His vital signs are healthy, and his general physical form is good," he continued, eyeing Yoshiko. "Wings are a little strangely made for a Nephan," he added. "Rather large and not so nipped in at the sides as you might expect. So he might not grow to be the fastest turner in the sky. More the kind of wings you'd see on an Alana dragon," he added.

The Alanas were formed to allow them to stay a long time in the air as they hovered over The Great Waters scouting for fish, whilst Nephans in contrast, usually had cropped wings which allowed them to manoeuvre rapidly in the sky.

The doctor tapped the underside of Yoshiko's wings.

"Some odd scales here," he said, pointing. "These seem like they haven't quite joined up with the rest of him."

Yoshiko had never noticed before, but now that he looked he had lots of rows of scales which pointed a little away from the wing rather than lying flat like they were supposed to. He closed his wings self-consciously.

"They won't affect his flying, but if you find your son doesn't like the look of them in a few years you can come and we'll get them clipped off," said the doctor.

He made a cutting motion with his talon and Kiara looked horrified.

"It's nothing to worry about" he continued, catching

her expression. "He might even grow into those wings and the odd hanging scales may just drop off. They almost look like little hooks don't they? But I imagine you're a good flyer already, aren't you?"

Yoshiko bowed his head modestly. He had been pleased with his attempt off the rock with Ketu, but he didn't like to show off.

The doctor put his equipment back into his desk and sat back.

"He is perhaps a little over sensitive," he said. "And you've fed him too much sticky mash," he said, pointing towards Yoshiko's rounded stomach. "This probably makes him all the more keen to prove himself with the other dragons."

Kiara looked guilty.

"I think what we are seeing is a condition where the scales lose a little of their colour" continued the doctor. "It can happen with young dragons if they are frequently upset. The different colour changes which you see are probably just a trick of the light."

Yoshiko opened his mouth to say something and then was silent again.

"You say you went orange when you were making fire? And purple in the presence of some Alana dragons?" said the doctor. "I expect what you saw was the reflection of the fire itself on your scales. And the second occasion, well, you were by a river which may have reflected the light back onto you."

Kiara looked bewildered. "He is a healthy red now,"

she said.

The doctor shook his head. "Scales can lose their colour sometimes and then return to normal," he said. "In almost all cases it is perfectly healthy and Yoshiko will grow out of it by the time he is older."

"But he changes colour." Insisted Kiara recalling Ketu's account. "Surely there is something odd about that?" But the doctor wasn't listening. He took out a stick of charcoal and began writing on a piece of paper. "Come back to me if there are any other problems," he said, as if signalling the conversation was closed.

Yoshiko hopped down off the desk and Kiara stood uncertainly. They left the doctor's surgery in silence, and both were hoping that what he'd said was true.

With his head lowered in thought Yoshiko crashed bodily into a plump violet stomach. He looked up apologetically to see a female Alana elder.

"Is this your son Kiara?" she said, not looking at Yoshiko.

"Hello Agna," said Kiara, her mind obviously still full of questions after their visit to the doctor. "And this must be little Igorr." she lowered her snout to greet a bored-looking hatchling standing beside his elder.

"Yes," said Agna. "But he causes me no end of trouble." she rolled her eyes as if Igorr wasn't with her. "That's why I'm here Kiara. The doctor gives me strong sleeping herbs. Otherwise I wouldn't get any sleep."

She gave a little toss of her head, and Igorr ducked his head down, refusing to look at anyone.

Kiara smiled thinly. "Come on Yoshiko," she said. "We'll go home and toast some dragon puffs on the fire." Yoshiko's face brightened. But he couldn't help wondering whether it really was Igorr's fault that his elder couldn't sleep well.

"Yoshiko, you must learn to quieten the clamour to be the greatest at fire and the fastest in the air, and listen to the voices inside yourself. Hear what they are trying to tell you."

Chapter Ten

Guya

During the seasons that followed Yoshiko learned to accept that he could sometimes change colour, and did his best to hide it from his fellow classmates at Fire School. He found that the colourations tended to happen when he was upset or emotional, and strove to keep his feelings from spilling out into his scales.

With the constant taunts and name-calling it wasn't easy, and he sometimes felt that the thing he'd learned best at Fire School was to hide away. Igorr knew that Yoshiko hid from him, and it made him all the more merciless on the few occasions when their paths met. Days at Fire School were a constant battle to hide his condition from the other pupils, and Yoshiko lived in constant fear that he would change colour publicly. Igorr had already seen him do it once and tried to spread the word, but to Yoshiko's relief the idea seemed too strange for the others to believe.

Yoshiko never told Ketu or Kiara when the different shades struck his scales, and privately he worried that the strange effects might never stop, despite what the doctor had said.

The hatchlings were now officially younglings,

and they could all fly and blow fire, but their scales were still soft and their claws short. Now he could fly himself to school and Yoshiko and Amlie went together, relishing the freedom of the skies. Like their elders, however, the younger dragons never flew over Cattlewick Cave on their way to Fire School, taking a longer route to avoid the solitary mountain. Every morning they tried to guess who or what the mysterious Guya might be, but neither had yet come up with a satisfactory answer.

"Perhaps he went to prison and was then banished from the clans" said Amlie. They had decided that the mysterious Guya must at the very least have super-strength, and most probably the power to change the thoughts of other dragons whilst they slept.

"Maybe he mixes up potions for dragons to give them good dreams," said Yoshiko, whose ideas were always on the imaginative side. "Perhaps he swims to the depths of The Great Waters every day to gather glitter-fish and uses them to decorate his cave."

"And he has the lungs of an Alana" agreed Amlie. "And the horn of a Talana for him to burrow his own rocks!"

They'd long since exhausted the general rumour about Guya, which was that he must have broken some law of Goadah, making him a bad dragon.

At school they trained once a week to make fire, and though Igorr teased him for his skills as a fire-blower, Yoshiko had regularly managed to make acceptable flames. Amlie was almost as good as an Effram dragon, and had trained herself to blow complicated shapes through each nostril. But when it came to making enormous fire balls which swallowed the target whole, none could beat Igorr.

Yoshiko had also made a new friend; a shy Mida dragon with huge dark eyes and long curled eyelashes called Cindina who sometimes flew to school with him and Amlie. She had warned him of a joke that Igorr and his friends had attempted to play on him by moving the target further away during his fire practice, and was disliked by the purple dragons as a result.

All three dragons ate their midday meal together, and were often joined by a green Effram male dragon named Elsy. Unlike the other hatchlings who tended to stick to their own clans in social situations the four made a colourful mixture of red, green and orange.

"What do you think of the Fire Pit training?" asked Elsy, as they munched on handfuls of stone-baked chips washed down with mineral juice. "Do you think they'll let us try out soon?"

Yoshiko looked out enviously to the Fire Pits at the front of the school, where they could just make out the peak of the flames which heated the cave to red-hot temperatures. The hatchlings had already toughened their skin without noticing during their fire-making practices, and none needed to rub themselves with whale-fruit for protection. Many young dragons visited the public Fire Pits with their parents near the Bushki clan village to strengthen their scales at the weekends. But though Ketu had offered to take him Yoshiko had been too embarrassed.

The truth was he felt shy of standing up on his haunches and exposing his round belly in front of the other dragons. And though he had sworn to practise until his skin was as thick as Ayo's on his first day of Fire School, he hadn't yet even started to train.

"The Fire Pits are full of Alanas," he said in reply.

Elsy nodded. "Not only Alanas though," he said. "Some other dragons are there too. Older ones from other clans."

Yoshiko was silent. He knew what Elsy was about to suggest.

"We should go and try it out," he said. "Try walking in the Fire Pit. The other clan dragons will make sure we get our turn. You don't need to worry about the Alanas."

Amlie gulped down her juice in excitement. "Are we allowed?" she said. "I didn't think we hatchlings were supposed to go in the Fire Pit until we're bigger."

Elsy shook his head. "The younger Alanas go every day," he said. "There are no rules that say we can't do it. But Ayo says it's at our own risk. Says he doesn't want the little dragons coming to him with scale-ache if they try it before they're ready."

Yoshiko looked at Elsy's scales, which were young looking, but somewhat toughened from his fire practice. As an Effram he had a natural ability with flame, and Yoshiko imagined that living with the other dragons of his clan Elsy was regularly exposed to the heat from the pot furnaces. He examined his own softer skin.

"Come on Yoshiko." Amlie was on her feet and tugging him up eagerly. Cindina looked worried. "I don't think I'll come along," she said, looking warily at Yoshiko as if to warn him away. "I don't know how well I can stand the heat. Besides, I want to keep my scales pretty." She tapped her delicate skin with a coy little smile.

Elsy took hold of Yoshiko's wing. "Come on Yoshiko!" he said. "Let's show those Alana dragons what we're made off!" Looking into his friend's faces Yoshiko didn't know what to do. Cindina was already retreating back into the school, but he didn't want to let Elsy and Amlie down. And they both seemed too excited.

"OK then," he said, forcing a smile. "But don't blame me if we all suffer the fire-aches tonight."

"No chance," said Elsy. "We've been blowing fire for months." And he raced off towards the Fire Pits, fanning out his wings to move him faster as he went. With a delighted look at Yoshiko, Amlie copied him, running across the main crescent. Unlike Cindina she had no worries about toughening up her scales.

The Fire Pits loomed on the other side of the crescent. They appeared dark and sinister-looking. Yoshiko remembered his first day at Fire School when he'd viewed the pits with excitement. He felt very differently now as he looked at the Alanas milling around the outside.

By the time they reached the Fire Pit entrance Yoshiko felt thoroughly sick, and wished he had stayed with Cindina. The only dragons trying out were much older than him, and looked huge in comparison, with leather-like scales. But what made it worse was Igorr and his two friends were there taking turns to wait it out in the flames, and when they saw Yoshiko a great sneer went up.

"Hey! It's little weedy Feddy who can't make fire!" said Igorr loudly, stepping out of the flames and still glowing with the heat. "Don't tell me you've come to show yourself up again and go crying home to Mummy, Nephan?"

"You're no Surion yourself!" retorted Elsy, narrowing his eyes at Igorr. "You're still only walking in the outside of the fire. And you're using whale fruit on your ears. In my clan even babies don't need that kind of protection."

Igorr frowned and was silent, and Yoshiko noticed his ears were indeed glistening with the tell-tale fruit. He looked to some of the older Nephan dragons, wondering if they would take an interest in defending a youngster from their own clan, but the burly dragons were striding purposely towards the hottest depths of the Pit, every muscle on their face deep in

126

concentration, and sweat pouring from their snouts.

"I'd like to see you do better Effram," said Igorr. But he didn't sound so certain now. Elsy grinned, and dropped his school net to the ground by Amlie. Then he walked calmly to the entrance and deliberately strode a path far deeper into the heart of the Fire Pit than the younger Alanas.

He emerged triumphant with only the slightest trickle of sweat on his upper lip.

Igorr set his mouth. "I'd like to see Feddy here walk the same path," he said. "The little Nephan has had so little contact with fire of his own that I'll bet he still needs to whale blubber his whole body when he practises making his little flames."

Yoshiko looked at him angrily, trying desperately to stay calm. He was having the feeling again. The sensation he got before he changed colour. And the last thing he wanted was for the dragons at school to realise his odd condition. It was also true that Kiara kept him away from their cave fire at home, so he was softer than most dragons his age.

"It's not a competition Igorr," he said. "I didn't come here to make a war of words with you. And you know that we Nephans don't have the naturally tough skin of the Effram dragons."

Igorr's mouth opened in a delighted smile. "He is afraid!" he crowed. "The loser Feddy has come to walk the Fire Pit and now he is too frightened!"

Amlie stepped forward. "He is not frightened to do

anything you could do Igorr," she said. "You couldn't walk the same route that Elsy just managed. Leave Yoshiko alone to walk the fire his own way."

By now many of the older dragons had stopped their own practice to watch the argument escalate between the little hatchlings. Some had even sat down to watch as they cooled down out of the fire.

Seizing the opportunity to humiliate Yoshiko further Igorr began a loud chant. "Walk! Walk! Walk! Come on Feddy! Show us you can manage to walk into the Fire Pit!"

His friends joined in, and Yoshiko was surrounded by the loud chanting. Something inside him began to fizz, and to his horror he realised he was changing colour. His claws were tinged yellow, but he knew that soon the shade would wash over his entire body. Everyone would see and the entire school would know what he was. A freak.

Yoshiko blinked his eyes, willing the colour to go away. And then he did the only thing he could think to do in the circumstances. He spread his wings and launched himself into the air, putting as much distance between himself and the Fire School as possible.

As he rose he could hear Igorr's taunts become louder and more victorious. They thought he was running away out of fear. But at least they wouldn't see his scales change. And as he turned, leaving the school far behind him, he looked to see he had changed to the bright yellow of a Bushki dragon.

Before he could help himself large tears began to fall, and with his eyes blurred he landed untidily on the nearest mountain. Yoshiko tried to take a deep breath to calm himself, but no calmness came, and instead he felt himself entirely overwhelmed with despair.

"My life is pointless," he said, suddenly, wondering at how true it all sounded when he said it out loud. A torrent of anger took hold of him and Yoshiko began pacing up and down, not caring who heard him. "I was the last in my clan to breathe fire," he said, as if checking off a list of his failures. "I am heavy and clumsy, and no good for anything. I can't even fly as fast as a Nephan should be able to, and now everyone at Fire School thinks I'm a coward."

More tears fell as he considered the unfairness of all this. What had he done to Igorr and his friends to deserve their treatment of him? He looked around to see that he had landed on an unfamiliar mountain. Dragor was full of such outposts, and most likely he could spend a few hours here alone without catching sight of another dragon. The idea of isolation appealed to him.

"There is no happiness ahead for me," he said, before collapsing back down on his haunches with a heavy sigh.

But to his great surprise his lament was met with an answer.

"That depends on how much happiness you are willing to make for yourself."

It was a low voice, old as the mountains but somehow young at the same time. Yoshiko looked around him in confusion. Had the mountain spoken?

"It's all very well to sit about feeling sorry for yourself" continued the voice. "But there are those less fortunate than you who manage to make the best for themselves."

Raising himself cautiously, Yoshiko rubbed away the tears and peered out into the distance. And then he saw him. A large red dragon carrying a basket of hand-picked herbs and roots.

"Who are you?" he said, momentarily forgetting his misery in the shock of seeing an elder away from his clan on this deserted mountain. His eyes widened to take in the sight. It was without a doubt the strangest dragon he'd ever seen. The scales were thick and greying to suggest great age, but unlike most elders this dragon had pronounced muscles all over his body, and the glistening turquoise eyes of a newborn. He looked like a hatchling and a youngling and an elder all in one. He was a Nephan red by colour, but it was the deepest clay red – almost another shade entirely from the rest of the clan, as if this dragon was a different species.

"Surely you have heard of me?" asked the dragon with a quizzical look. "This is my mountain after all. I am Guya."

Yoshiko backed away uncertainly.

"I... I am sorry," he said, the rules of never landing on Guya's mountain turning his stomach in fear. "I'll leave you. Leave you alone now."

But Guya shook his head slowly, as if he had all the time in the world. "Don't be in such a hurry little dragon," he said. "It has been so long since I've had company that I should not mind the conversation of a smalling. And besides you may have more of a purpose here than you think."

Even more now, Yoshiko wanted to get away. The older dragon was speaking in riddles, and he talked like a Commandment of Goadah. No one used words like 'smalling' anymore.

But Guya seemed to be able to read his thoughts. "There is no need to be alarmed," he said, with a kindly expression. "You are quite safe here. But I think you have come to learn something."

Yoshiko shook his head. "I came by accident," he explained. "I couldn't see well because... because..." he stopped, not wanting to admit he had been crying.

"Because your eyes were filled with tears?" asked Guya.

Yoshiko nodded, unable to help himself welling up again. "I am the worst at Fire School!" he cried suddenly. "Many hate me, and I can't fly properly, or breathe fire, or do anything a dragon like me should be able to do!" And he stuck out his lower lip in grief at the thought.

Guya had seemed kindly, and Yoshiko had rather expected from his manner that he might put out a comforting wing, but to his surprise the elder simply looked at him coolly and then motioned for him to follow.

"Come come," said Guya. "Better we talk about such things in the cave. You wouldn't want anyone else to hear you feeling so sorry for yourself," he added.

Yoshiko shut his mouth in annoyance. What could the old dragon know about what he'd gone through? He didn't have to attend Fire School every day with Igorr and the rest.

"I imagine you're wondering what an old dragon could know of Fire School" chuckled Guya, demonstrating once again an alarming tendency to read his thoughts. "But I went to Fire School once, just as you do now, and things do not change very much."

"Come then," he added, seeing Yoshiko's reluctance to follow him. "Better we talk in the cave."

They rounded the mountain path and a large craggy entrance revealed itself, far grander than Yoshiko's family cave. He stared up in wonder at the lofty opening. Having only seen Cattlewick Cave from the air he hadn't realised quite how large it was up close.

"Not bad for an old dragon eh?" said Guya, noticing his awe. "I had two very talented Talanas extend this cave for me over forty seasons ago, and it still looks as grand as it ever did."

As they walked through the large entrance area however, the cave became smaller, and to Yoshiko's delight the walls closed around them in a maze of colourful crystal. All kinds of glittering minerals grew from the stone in pinks and greens and blues and purples. The effect was like a fairy grotto, sparkling with precious stones.

A smell of smoking herbs wafted out at them, and small torches made the dwelling seem inviting. And as they turned into the main body of the cave, Yoshiko saw that bookcases lined the wall. He looked around in amazement. He had never seen so much written material. Heavy ancient books and paper covered in charcoal writing. Much of it was in symbols which Yoshiko had never read before, not even in Fire School.

In the centre of it all was the most complicated set of cauldrons he'd ever seen. A large copper centrepiece was joined by glass tubes and bubbling pans and pots, all apparently in the act of making a herbal concoction of some kind.

"My special sorrel juice," said Guya, catching his eye. "You won't find anything like it in all of Dragor. Puts extra fire in your belly and metal in your wings," he added, strolling over to the pot, and adding a careful assortment of the herbs from his basket.

"Many dragons have forgotten the proper way to make sorrel juice," he said as the extra herbs threw out smoke from the pan. "Not enough time, make it too simple. The old ways are the best." And as if to prove this he drew off a little cup for himself and took a long draught with a happy sigh.

"Try some," he added, holding the cup out towards his guest. And hesitantly Yoshiko took it. It looked a lot like the ordinary sorrel juice he had at home, he thought, looking suspiciously into the container. But there was something else about it. Like gold and silver dancing on the surface of the liquid.

Seeing Guya's face he took a polite sip. And then as it flowed over his tongue he made another gulp. It was like fire and ice all at once and bitter but sweet. Tasting it felt like some kind of balance had been restored. The despair from earlier settled and then he felt lifted.

"Good stuff?" asked Guya. And without waiting for an answer, he settled himself down, and eyed the younger dragon critically. "The best sorrel juice you'll drink though will be that you make for yourself," he said.

Yoshiko didn't know how to reply. He'd never helped Kiara make sorrel juice, but he couldn't understand why it would make any difference who made it.

"So what do you mean by it then?" asked Guya. "All this crying over nothing and feeling sorry for yourself? You're not a baby hatchling any more."

Rather shocked by the tone, Yoshiko stumbled to defend himself. "I... There are dragons who pick on me at school," he explained. "Today in the Fire Pit. And I can't fly as fast as the other dragons. My fire rarely hits the target... and," he stopped, wondering whether to tell Guya. But something about the cave made him feel safe. "I change colour," he whispered. "When things happen to make me upset. My scales change."

It felt like a great relief to tell another dragon, and he realised he hardly cared whether Guya met this piece of news with the same matter-of-fact manner. Just saying it out loud felt so much better.

Rather than frown, however, Guya's face softened, and he grunted kindly. "I don't know what it is, this colour changing," he said. "I confess I have never heard of any dragon doing such a thing before. But then again what is so wrong with it?"

Yoshiko blinked. "I'm... I'm different." he said, raising his voice a little. Clearly Guya wasn't quite grasping what he was saying. The older dragon shuffled comfortably. "Who isn't different," he said simply, continuing to gaze straight ahead. "And what a terrible place it would be if we were all the same."

"It's not just a bit different," protested Yoshiko. "It's not like a Talana with a large horn or an Alana with a fat snout."

"And all the better for that I should think," said Guya. "It sounds like a special gift which you have there." He tipped himself another cup of sorrel juice. "Everything you need is already inside of you," he continued. "The talent... the gifts you need, and the

135

knowledge of how to use those gifts. Seems your only problem is you've found one and not the other Yoshiko."

Yoshiko started, wondering how the dragon knew his name.

"I have a feeling you have a purpose" Guya continued. "Each dragon has a purpose, but yours may be more unusual than most. It is every dragon's mission in life to discover their individual purpose, but yours may also be harder to find. But you must trust that everything you are now going through is part of that higher purpose and learning. You will find it."

For a brief moment Yoshiko felt assured. It was as though Guya had seen into his soul and mapped out a life of significance. But then he remembered the reality of his situation and anger set in.

"I don't need a higher purpose!" he said. "I don't want one, and I never asked for one. I just want to be like everybody else!"

Guya settled on him a gentle look.

"I know how you feel," he said. "I was the same as you Yoshiko. I was also confused. I also rebelled against my true identity, and wanted to be normal like the other dragons. It is only with wisdom we learn that normal is meaningless."

"It must be my purpose to fail," said Yoshiko. Not caring that he was being rude. "What other purpose could I have? I fail at everything I attempt."

"You certainly are very good at thinking yourself a

hard done by little dragon," said Guya. "What makes you think it is worse for you than anyone else?"

"It is worse!" said Yoshiko with feeling. "Everyone else can fly, and can breathe fire."

"And so can you," said Guya simply. "It is of no matter that you are not the best at some skills. You have other gifts. And if you'd only stop paying so much attention to how your talents are not the same as the others then you might discover them all the more quickly."

"What gifts? What do you mean?" Yoshiko was curious despite himself.

"I cannot tell you what makes you special Yoshiko or what talent you may have, or what you have to give to Dragor and your fellow dragons," said Guya. "That is for you to learn." he paused for a moment. "But I may be able to help you if you are willing to trust."

"Trust what?" asked Yoshiko.

"Yourself of course," said Guya. "You must trust that the answers are all inside you already. You are looking outside for answers to your questions, grasping for what you do not have. But the way is to look inside, and learn to know what you have already. Yoshiko you must learn to quieten the clamour to be the greatest at fire and the fastest in the air, and listen to the voices inside yourself. Hear what they are trying to tell you."

Yoshiko looked back in confusion. What inner voices? Surely hearing voices inside your head was a bad thing, not a good one. But something told him to listen to Guya. After all, he thought, he couldn't feel much worse than he did already.

"Alright," he said, taking a step forward. "Tell me what it is I must do. Can you give me a potion?"

Guya laughed. "You have heard too many Surion-tales," he said. "You carry with you all you need for happiness wherever you go. And you do not need any special place or thing to bring it out. All you need to do is listen."

Yoshiko closed his eyes impatiently. "OK. I'm listening. Now what?"

Guya took his wing gently, and Yoshiko opened his eyes again. "I mean really listen," said Guya. "Become still and listen."

Yoshiko looked confused, and Guya smiled at him. "You remind me so much of myself as a younger dragon," he said. Then he got up from his haunches and placed the sorrel cup carefully in its place. Everything he did was considered, thought Yoshiko. As if he had trained in some ancient art.

"Come with me," said Guya, beckoning him up once again. And mesmerised, Yoshiko followed.

"Where are we going?" he asked. But Guyu tutted and waved him to silence. They wove out through the sparkling cave of gemstones and back out onto the mountain. Everything seemed different now, Yoshiko thought. Like some new dawn outside the cave. Guya had disappeared ahead of him and he had to work to keep up. He rounded the corner and the old dragon was already vanishing around another curve of the large mountain.

Yoshiko chased behind, not looking where he was going in his haste to keep up, and as he turned past the corner where Guya had disappeared, he smacked bodily into the bulk of the other dragon.

"Have a care," said Guya. But he sounded less testy now. "Look where you are going." Yoshiko mumbled an apology, but Guya raised a single claw to silence him. "Look," he said slowly "where you are going." And in an elegant sweep of his talons he gestured out before him.

Yoshiko looked out in amazement. He had hardly noticed the landscape in his rush. But as he looked up he saw The Great Waters before him, but from an angle he'd never seen before. From this part of Dragor the waters glinted like they were filled with gold as the sun's intensity penetrated through the mist of smoke that protected them. The sweep of the liquid seemed endless. He whistled appreciatively and Guya chuckled.

"You see Yoshiko," he said. "There is so much beauty all around us, and so few stop to look for it."

"I've never seen The Great Waters from here before" breathed Yoshiko. "It makes them look so..."

"So beautiful?" asked Guya. "The Great Waters are beautiful wherever you look. But you are looking at them in a different way."

Yoshiko frowned, but Guya didn't seem to feel the

need to explain himself, and instead closed his eyes.

"So much beauty," he repeated.

Not quite knowing what to do Yoshiko sat close to the old dragon who seemed to be almost in a trance. He watched as the breath came slowly from the great chest and peered curiously at the great scaly eyelids.

Guya opened a single eye and looked down at Yoshiko. "Feel the water," he said. "It has special qualities." But Yoshiko looked back confused. "You want me to dive into the water?" he asked. Guya shook his head. "Feel it," he said. "In your scales. Listen to it. The Great Waters are at the heart of Dragor. They nourish us. Provide us with food, with life."

Obediently Yoshiko closed his eyes, but for what reason he wasn't sure. Then he heard Guya's voice coming calmly from beside him. "Imagine the waters before you," he said. "Flowing up. Delivering life."

But Yoshiko's thoughts raced again. If anyone from the Fire School could see him now, seated with the old dragon staring out onto The Great Waters with his eyes closed... It didn't bear thinking about.

Guya's voice came crossly this time. "Do not be so quick to worry what others think of you" he said. "You are not yet grown and have no need for such silly thoughts."

Yoshiko screwed up his eyes tight.

"Relax," said Guya. "Let your scales become soft." And as he said it Yoshiko felt as though something warm and comforting was passing through him. He untightened his expression and tried to picture what the waters were like in front of him.

A slow steady heat seemed to build in his feet and it began to course through him steadily. It felt strangely familiar. Guya's voice was approving. "Good," he said. "You are getting the feel for it."

Yoshiko concentrated harder and the sensation passed all over, rippling from his forehead to the claws of his feet. He smiled slightly to himself luxuriating in the feeling.

Then he made the mistake of opening his eyes.

To his shock he was as dark blue as a Saiga dragon from head to toe. Yoshiko gasped in shock. "Now," said Guya, who was staring at him gently. "Let it all go."

Trying not to panic at the embarrassment of another dragon seeing his colour change Yoshiko breathed out in one steady breath, and to his amazement the colour vanished gracefully from his body, returning his scales to a healthy Nephan red.

Beside him Guya nodded. "So you have witnessed your gift of colour change," he said. "It is as I thought." And he rose to his feet as if no more needed to be said on the subject, and began to walk back to the entrance of his cave.

Wide eyed in shock Yoshiko ran after him.

"Wait!" he called, as Guya rounded the curve in the mountain. "How did you? Did you do that?"

Guya didn't turn around but he smiled a little.

"I've never been able to control it" explained

Yoshiko, struggling to keep pace with the elderly dragon. "The colour changing I mean. Do you... Do you know how to make the colour changing stop?"

Guya stopped. "I do not know how to make the colour changing go away," he said. And Yoshiko's face fell. "But I do know how to help you to discover how to control it"

Yoshiko felt a sudden flush of relief. "Will you show me? Show me how to keep control of the colours?"

He was delighted. For the first time since he'd started Fire School the chance of being a normal dragon was ahead of him. It didn't matter if he started to change colour if he could learn the power of how to make the different shades go away if he wanted to. No one would even notice.

But Guya's face had lost some of its warmth,

"I will not teach you," he said. "I said I would help you and I did. I showed you the gift you already have. But beyond that I will do no more."

Yoshiko's mouth dropped open in horror. "But... Why not?" he asked.

"You are not ready for teaching," said Guya.

Yoshiko was crestfallen. How could he make the dragon teach him?

"Please," he said, his lower lip trembling. "Please help me. I'll do anything. I'll sweep your cave every day if I have to."

Guya rested a wing on his shoulder. "I sense many things about you Yoshiko. I think perhaps you could have some great thing to bring to Dragor. But now you are too young. All you care about is what other dragons think about you."

"You don't know what it's like," said Yoshiko. "They tease me."

Guya raised a warning talon. "And you think you can change how happy you feel," he pressed his claw to his heart, "if others would only treat you differently." The wing reached out expansively, and Guya shook his head sadly. "All wrong, all backward little dragon. You must master what is on the inside first."

Yoshiko scowled. "How can I possibly be happy when the others are picking on me?" he shouted.

"They cannot be truly happy if they are picking on you either," said Guya. "You want to make the largest fire, to spend the longest time in the Fire Pit. But life isn't like that. Spend your life proving yourself to others and you will have an empty space. In life the only true mission is to find out how to use the gifts you already have. That is how you gain the respect of other dragons."

Guya's face softened just a little. "I cannot teach you," he repeated. "You are not ready. Maybe in three winters little one, you will have learned the blessing of your gift."

"I think three winters is the minimum!" Yoshiko was outraged. "I'll have been laughed out of Fire School by that time."

"Three winters is the minimum" Guya retorted. "If

143

you want to spend your days feeling sorry for yourself it could be ten."

Yoshiko opened and shut his mouth, desperate to try and think of an answer that would persuade Guya to help him control his colour changing sooner.

"Can I come back and see you?" he said finally. "I mean. Can I visit? And sit with you? And look onto The Great Waters?"

Guya coughed dismissively. "Looking onto The Great Waters is not for every day," he said. "It is a special day. A special mood." he paused, just for a second. "Tomorrow is sorrel juice day," he said. "If you learn the talent well enough to make your own batch of sorrel juice then it is said you will learn all the secrets of your own heart. Perhaps this is a way for you to find out what your gift is for."

Yoshiko grasped the opportunity. "Can I come and learn with you?" he said. "To make the juice?"

They had reached the opening of the cave now, and Yoshiko knew instinctively that he would not be invited back inside. The visit to Guya's private world was over. "Much work to make sorrel juice the right way," said the old dragon. "Not just gathering of a few herbs and throwing in a pot. To make good sorrel juice takes time."

"I've got time!" blurted Yoshiko. "Let me help. I'll prove to you that I can do it. That I can make great sorrel juice."

Guya shook his head. "So fast, so fast," he said. "It

takes many many winters to make the right sorrel juice. Again you are too quick."

"I'll come back tomorrow," said Yoshiko determinedly. "I'll bring you the best sorrel leaves in Dragor, you'll see."

This time Guya looked more interested. "You are persistent at least," he said. "And perhaps this is something which can grow to the good. Bring me the best sorrel tomorrow and yes alright then, we will start early, before Fire School to make the juice. Then we will see how things are done. If you succeed you may one day make the sorrel juice for yourself and learn much about your own gifts. But you may never learn the art."

Yoshiko nodded, feeling strangely exhilarated. "I won't let you down," he said. "I'll bring you the best there is, you'll see."

Yoshiko's family had gathered sorrel from the same part of Dragor for generations, and Ketu had often boasted to his son that they had access to the best sorrel patch in all the land that only a few dragons knew of. Usually they only visited this particular patch on special occasions such as New Birth's Eve, or Red Seventh Moon. But the next morning Yoshiko got up before the sun rose to fly out to the special patch.

"Where are you going," asked Ketu sleepily, eyeing his son's enthusiastic munching on a bowl of peat porridge. "It's not even sun up."

145

"I'm going to do some training" said Yoshiko "Some from school do early training so they can be an asset to Dragor," he added withholding the detail.

Ketu grinned. "I remembered doing something similar at your age. Don't give yourself scale-ache Yoshiko." He said, presuming he meant at the Fire Pit. And he turned back over in his perch.

Having eaten his morning food Yoshiko stretched his wings and launched off into the dark morning.

He had never been out of the cave this early, and there was something almost mystical in the fresh air of Dragor's dawn. Already some of the Alanas were gathered around their fishing spots on The Great Waters, eager to bring about the best catch of the day before the fish were more alive to their skills. And the hard-working Efframs had already fired up their ovens to make clay pots.

Yoshiko wheeled in the sky, taking in the various scenes, before heading to the Sorrel Grove by the deserted mountains next to the Saiga clan. He settled here carefully. Anxiety seized him suddenly. He had never been here alone before, and realised he would have no-one to ask about how to do things. Usually Kiara or Ketu always explained things and began the harder work first, leaving him to bundle up the leaves. Taking a deep breath he tried to stay calm, reminding himself why he was here. You can do this. He whispered to himself. It's only picking sorrel.

Yoshiko followed the well-worn track to his family's famous sorrel patch. The leaves were thorny and bright green, and he moved in uncertainly before beginning to strip down the branches and loading them into his net. Like all the best sorrel the plants were stiff and difficult to take, but he worked solidly and soon he was sweating with the effort. What made it worse was that he was sure he was doing it wrongly somehow without Ketu or Kiara to look over him.

Yoshiko looked at the little net. It was far less than the family gathered for last New Birth's Eve, but at that time of year they were harvesting enough of the special herb to make cauldrons of festive juice for weeks at a time. He felt sure this would be enough for one old dragon's daily cauldron. He launched himself back in the air and headed for Guya's cave.

He landed unsteadily with the unfamiliar weight of the herbs, and as he settled himself he saw Guya was already waiting for him. The dragon must have risen at dawn, he realised.

"Is this all the sorrel you have brought?" Guya motioned to the little net, and Yoshiko nodded.

"Is it right?" he asked. "Did I pick the right ones?"

"It is good green sorrel," said Guya.

Yoshiko let out a sigh of relief. He felt strangely exhilarated to realise he had done it all by himself.

Guya grunted. "Did it take you a long time?" he said.

"I was up before sunrise," said Yoshiko. Guya took

the net without a word, and his thick talons delved into the sorrel. He ground some between his claws, and took a deep sniff.

"When I was young like you I would rise before dawn to gather the best sorrel, but I did not arrive to grind the sorrel before the sun was much higher than it is now." He gestured up to the sky that seemed clearer in this part of Dragor. It was a beautiful spot, he thought, this isolated mountain. Whenever he had flown over it on the way to Fire School Yoshiko had looked down on Guya's Mountain as a deserted place, but now he could appreciate why the older dragon might enjoy living here.

Yoshiko frowned however. He had come all the way down here at dawn, but still his efforts seemed unappreciated. For a moment he seriously considered flying away and never coming back. And then he remembered Fire School the day before. He already had a day of taunting to look forward to. He wasn't going to give up on his chance to control his colour changing now.

"Come," said Guya. "We will see what can be done. It is good sorrel that you bring at least." And he gave another appreciative sniff.

Reluctantly now, Yoshiko followed him into the cave. The sparkling walls of gems looked different in the morning light. The colours were softer and they flashed gently as Yoshiko followed Guya.

The main body of the cave looked different too. The

bubbling cauldron which had been over the fire the day before was cleaned and set away, and instead an array of blue stone bowls were laid out.

Yoshiko had seen this kind of equipment before. Kiara had a bowl that she'd inherited from her elder and she took it out for occasions when she and Ketu wanted to make a particularly special limestone pie. But for the purposes of making normal sorrel juice Yoshiko had never seen the old stone bowls.

Guya indicated that the younger dragon should settle himself by one of the bowls and Yoshiko sat down, looking up questioningly.

"Where is the fire?" he asked. But Guya simply threw a talon full of strange looking herbs into the bowl in front of Yoshiko. "Grind them" he said simply.

"But… How?" asked Yoshiko. "What do I do?"

"You do not need an elder to tell you how to do a hatchling job," said Guya. "You must get on with the work. Wings need less answers than ears."

Yoshiko had heard this phrase before. It meant that it was faster to learn by doing than by explanation. He'd always had things clearly spelled out to him before.

"What if I do it wrong?" he said, worrying that he might ruin an entire batch of sorrel juice for the day.

"A mistake doesn't matter, like a fire target you miss, or a test you need to take again, you keep going until you get it right," said Guya, and before Yoshiko could ask him anything else he turned and left.

Yoshiko picked up the little grinding stone by his

bowl and started to mash up the herbs. At first he pounded nervously, waiting to see if the older dragon would come back with more instructions. But after a few minutes he got on with the work, and soon he realised he was working unaided. Guya had been right after all.

Still it seemed to be taking forever. Despite using all the power of his arms the herbs seemed to be hardly mashing up at all. Some had pods and seeds attached. He tried lifting the grinder and smashing it back down to break them up. It was hard work, and within a few minutes tiny beads of sweat were running down his snout. But he wouldn't give up, and after thirty solid minutes of work the herbs began to give up their fragrant innards to the bowl.

Yoshiko had never hung around to watch Kiara and Ketu make the sorrel juice and didn't realise how much work was involved. If he was going to be an elder himself one day he should pay more attention, he thought.

After the herbs were properly ground Guya appeared again from nowhere and threw another large handful into the bowl.

"More?" Yoshiko was aghast. The contents of the bowl were now more than double what they had been at the start. But Guya had vanished again. With a sigh of annoyance Yoshiko picked up the grinder and started again. Smoke began to filter back to where he was sitting and he thought a fire was being made to boil the sorrel. At least things were getting started now.

After another twenty minutes Guya had returned, but this time rather than adding more to Yoshiko's bowl he beckoned with his claw that he should stand. Yoshiko wiped his brow in relief. Finally it was time to get started on making the juice. And then he could finally learn the technique of how to stop his skin from changing colour.

But rather than leading him to the cauldron Guya instead walked back out to the front of the cave.

"It is time for you to go to Fire School," said Guya, pointing to where the sun was in the sky. "You will make it in plenty of time. Always better to be early," he added thoughtfully.

Yoshiko's mouth fell open in amazement. "But... But we were making sorrel juice," he protested. "And you were going to teach me how to control my..." he stopped before saying the words out loud. "The thing that happens with my scales," he finished lamely.

"You did not grind the herbs fast enough," said Guya. "And I cannot have you being late for your schooling – your training with the other dragons." he stopped to choose his words. "One day you will be faster with the herbs. When you are faster then you may help with the boiling. When you master the boiling then we have the special way to drink the sorrel juice. It must be with the right respect to the ancient ones, our departed dragons. Once you have mastered all of these things then perhaps you will be ready to master yourself, your own gifts, and understand how to have the right respect for them."

"Guya, you said that if I made the sorrel juice I'd understand… what happens with the colour changing." Yoshiko wanted to be clear what he was working for. But Guya only shook his head.

"I said it might tell you what your gifts are for." He said. "Making the sorrel juice – it takes a long time to learn the skill, and my sorrel juice is special. It is made only with the right herbs and the right processes. As I said before, drink it and you may be granted insights into yourself. This may tell you more about your gift. But there are no guarantees."

"How long will that take?" Yoshiko was adding up the days until he hoped to have himself in check.

Guya shrugged. "How long does anything take?" he said. "The lesson is over when the student is ready for the next. But I cannot say how long it will be. Work hard Yoshiko, and the lesson will be learned sooner. That is all I can tell you."

"But what if it takes many winters?" Yoshiko was wondering whether it was worth bothering with. All this effort and he hadn't even got to boiling the sorrel yet. After his morning's work his claws were sore and there were blisters on his palms.

He didn't know how long it would be before he could grind the herbs fast enough to boil the sorrel in time to get to Fire School – maybe weeks. It could be even longer.

"It's too long!" he said to Guya. "How can I go to school? Everybody hates me! I need to control my skin or it will get worse."

For the first time that day Guya smiled at him. "You are saying you don't have friends at school?" he said.

Yoshiko hesitated. He knew he had friends. Amlie was his best friend, and Elsy was also becoming closer to him.

"I do have friends," he admitted. "But not all the dragons like me. There are lots who think I am a baby because I can't make fire as well as others. And I can't do things as well as I would like because I am frightened of changing colour."

Guya shook his head. "It sounds as if you are feeling sorry for yourself again," he said. "Not every dragon is liked by every other dragon. Surion himself had many enemies." he paused and looked out into the distance as if he was remembering something.

"Can't you show me faster?" asked Yoshiko, taking the moment of Guya's reflection to test how far he might be able to push the teaching process.

"No-one can make life happen any faster," said Guya. "But you don't have to come here. Helper for sorrel juice, no helper for sorrel juice. I have been alone a long long time. It makes no difference to me." He locked his turquoise eyes with Yoshiko's just for a moment.

"If you want to have a better time at school I suggest

you learn to ignore these dragons who don't like you." he said, and then he retreated back into his cave.

"How can I ignore them!" Yoshiko shouted after him. "They follow me round, calling me names!"

"Ignore them for long enough," said Guya, without looking back. "And they'll stop following you."

Yoshiko kicked a patch of dust in annoyance as Guya vanished into his cave. How could he ignore them? It was so unfair. A little voice rose up in his head, that maybe he should try. He dismissed it instantly. When he managed to gain control of his colour changing, then he could be like everyone else and the others would leave him alone.

And with a lot on his mind Yoshiko took off into the sky, on his way to Fire School.

When Yoshiko landed he was one of the first arrivals, and he looked around at the empty courtyard. Guya was right in a way, he thought. It was a different feeling to have plenty of time to think about the day ahead. Usually he and Amlie spilled into school, racing through the stone tunnels to get to their lessons on time. Yoshiko wandered over to the Fire Pit, which now stood completely empty. The thought occurred to him that if he got in early enough he would have the entire pit to himself to train. It looked as though even the much older dragons preferred not to get off their perches too early.

He waited while the courtyard gradually filled with other dragons, feeling his mind working slowly on his problems as he saw them. The truth was he liked Guya. The old dragon might be difficult and mysterious in his answers to questions. But he had a calmness about him which was good to be around. He saw Amlie on the skyline, and realised he didn't have long with his own thoughts. In a quick moment he decided he would go back to see Guya. At least for another few days. If he didn't get any faster at grinding the sorrel then he would stop. It was simple. And if everything went wrong and he never learned anything, then maybe the doctors would be able to do something a second time around. He grimaced at the thought of having to ask a worried Kiara to take him to the herb doctor. For the time being at least, he thought he would try to do things his own way.

"You dared come back to school then?"

Igorr's voice echoed through the crescent suddenly. Yoshiko groaned inwardly. He turned to see the other dragon but didn't reply.

"Everyone saw you run away," gloated Igorr. "You're useless, useless Feddy. You can't do anything right."

A spasm of fear passed through Yoshiko. He usually managed to avoid Igorr in the morning but it looked like he was going to have to face him.

"Leave him alone Igorr," said Amlie.

Yoshiko thought back to Guya's advice, and rather than replying as he would normally have done he turned round to Amlie as if Igorr didn't exist.

"Are you deaf?" spat Igorr. But Yoshiko said nothing. Instead he started talking to Amlie about the day's lesson ahead.

"We all know you'll never make the Fire Pit," continued Igorr, but Yoshiko screwed up his talons and resisted saying anything back.

It wasn't easy to keep his concentration with taunts shouted at him, but eventually the other dragon went away. Yoshiko looked down to see his claws were shaking.

"Come on," said Amlie. "Let's get to class."

The rest of the day passed in something of a daze, but at the end of school Igorr and his fellow Alanas still followed Yoshiko around the crescent laughing at his earlier cowardice. He sighed to himself. Guya's suggestion obviously hadn't worked.

By the time he returned home he'd almost forgotten that he hadn't told Ketu who he was visiting that morning.

"How was the Fire Pit?" asked Ketu, and Yoshiko waited almost a full minute before he remembered his father's parting words.

It didn't feel good not to be open with his elders, and Yoshiko resolved he would soon tell Ketu and Kiara all about Guya. But he would wait a few days. That way if helping the old dragon came to nothing he wouldn't have to explain to his elders everything about his recent colour change and where he had been escaping off to in the early mornings.

"Have a lot on your mind?" asked Ketu in response to Yoshiko's silence and remembering the trouble with Igorr at school. "Yes much on my mind" Yoshiko simply replied, before walking off towards his fire target. Today had been a long day. His meeting with Igorr had not been so bad, but tomorrow he had every intention of waiting until the line of dragons waiting to go into class had filed in before running in to join them. That way he avoided having to stand near Igorr and the other Alanas.

"I've been thinking Yoshiko," said Ketu. "It's time you told one of your teachers about this problem with Igorr."

Yoshiko looked in horror. The last thing he wanted to do was report Igorr. Surely that would only make things worse. But Ketu was insistent.

"Why don't you just try it?" he said. "You might be surprised. Dragons like Igorr might seem very brave when no elders are around, but they are always very scared of the teachers."

"What if it makes things worse?" he asked.

"I don't think it will," said Ketu. "Why don't you try it?"

The idea of telling his teachers about Igorr was still on Yoshiko's mind the next morning as he gathered sorrel for Guya until his net was bursting. He was pleased to find that the picking process seemed much faster this morning. Maybe the act of grinding the herb would be the same, he thought, as he took flight towards the lonely mountain.

He arrived at Guya's cave to find the old dragon was nowhere to be seen, and feeling slightly anxious at entering uninvited he peered cautiously into the glittering interior. He could hear some banging about in the back, and he crept slowly forward.

"Guya?"

The question was met with a coughing. "Come in, come in" he beckoned. "There is no need to wait for me to greet you every morning. You can come in and do things on your own." Relieved Yoshiko continued into the back of the cave.

"I've brought more sorrel," he said, as Guya's red scales came into view. "What is that?" The older dragon was clutching an enormous book in his hands, full of pictures of creatures which Yoshiko had never seen before. Perched on his nose was a set of crystal reading goggles, and Guya glanced up at Yoshiko from behind enormous eyes.

"This? These are humans Yoshiko." His talon traced the outline of a strange shaped animal standing upright on two legs.

Yoshiko peered closer. "They look so strange."

"Yes they do." said Guya. "And many dragons think they're an evil kind of species. But humans are special in their own way Yoshiko. They don't teach you much at school about the land outside Dragor, but once the dragons shared it with humans. It's bigger than you could ever imagine – further across than you could ever fly, with animals and plants which would make your scales curl and your eyes pop out of your head."

Yoshiko's eyes widened. Had Guya seen the land outside Dragor? He didn't dare ask.

So he said instead: "Do you think humans are an evil species?"

Guya closed the book with a snap. "This is too complicated for dragons who have not even made sorrel yet. But we will see Yoshiko. Perhaps one day I shall explain to you some of its contents. Now," he stood. "Are you ready to pound more herbs?"

Yoshiko nodded with an enthusiasm he didn't feel. Suddenly the idea of Guya training him to discover the secrets of his colour changing seemed like an impossible dream. Perhaps he was just a cranky old dragon who wanted someone to make his sorrel juice for him. And given his way of making it took so much longer than any other dragon family Yoshiko knew, maybe it was time he found a better recipe. But thinking back to tasting the finished juice Yoshiko had to admit it had a finer flavour than any he had tasted.

When Guya wandered over to add more herbs to the bowl he decided to ask his advice on his problem with Igorr.

"Ketu says I should tell my teachers about the dragons who tease me at school," he said. "But you said I should ignore them."

Guya nodded slowly. "Both good advice," he said. "First gets fast results which end as quickly. One takes longer, is harder, and if you do it right it lasts forever."

Yoshiko rolled his eyes. Guya was talking in puzzles.

"What should I do to end the problem now," he insisted.

Guya shrugged. "Tell your teachers," he said. But Yoshiko had a feeling there was something more to what he was saying.

He went back angrily to his stone bowl pounding away, and after ten minutes it almost felt as though he'd never left. Yoshiko wiped a line of sweat away, quietly telling himself that this was the last morning. It was too much like hard work he thought.

When he landed at Fire School that morning Yoshiko decided it was time to follow Ketu's advice. He was tired of avoiding the other dragons and hiding from Igorr. And besides, he thought, the problem couldn't get any worse. So instead of waiting outside the class he went in early to speak to Ma'am Sancy.

"I've been wondering when you'd come to me," she said, after listening to his problem. "I can't help you unless you tell me the problem. But now you have I will talk to Igorr and tell him to stop calling you names."

Yoshiko felt relieved. Secretly he had been thinking that his story wouldn't be believed, and that the teacher would refuse to help. But true to her word at the end of class she called Igorr to one side as the other dragons left.

He never knew what the teacher said, but sure enough Igorr stopped calling him Feddy in front of the other dragons, and his friends stopped their taunts as well. Yoshiko felt the happiest he'd been since he started Fire School, although he knew that Igorr still hated him, and the purple dragons glared after him as he came into School.

Cattlewick Cave had become Yoshiko's most fascinating place and almost addictive, and despite his tired thoughts to stay away from the hard work he felt compelled to come back the next morning, and the next. And as the mid year heat of Dragor slowly turned to a cooler temperature Yoshiko rose shivering whilst it was still dark to gather the sorrel leaves. He couldn't really explain what made him to go back and help Guya. Only that it had become a comfortable habit to rise, gather sorrel, and pound it to a sticky paste in the cave. Now that the mornings were cooler Guya often greeted him with a hot berry water, or a few honey cakes. And whatever he was given to eat or drink was always delicious. Yoshiko was getting faster at pounding the sorrel, he knew. But nowhere near as fast as he had hoped. Whilst he had expected to be twice as fast by the second day and then twice as fast again by the next, the progress had been extremely slow.

He had not even noticed that he had improved at all until finally Guya said. "You are a little faster. I have given you a few extra herbs this last week."

Something had also changed in him during his mornings in the cave. Somehow it didn't matter so much that he might never achieve the result he had been hoping for. He felt a sense of achievement that he could do it all alone without an elder looking over him. It was enough that he rose early, gathered the herbs and ground them up in the calming company of Guya. He liked the way that Dragor was almost empty of life as he took to the skies before dawn, with only a few other dragons sharing the secret with him of their beautiful land. And he had come to enjoy the constant movement of his grinding stone against the bowl, '*tuk tuk tuk*' as it reduced the sorrel to a paste.

He was different at Fire School too, and even his friends noticed it. Yoshiko had more faith in himself.

"You never ask for help anymore," said Amlie, as Yoshiko filled out his slab carefully with the charcoal pencil. "Before, you had to check with the teacher that everything you did was right. You were always scared of getting something wrong. Now you hardly ever ask."

"Wings need less answers than ears," said Yoshiko, as he carefully filled out his book. "Sometimes it's better just to get on with things and learn that way."

And then, just a few months later something amazing happened.

Elsy had insisted they all go back to the Fire Pit to try out their skill, and Yoshiko was dreading it, knowing that the Alanas would be there. Amlie had tried to persuade Elsy to do something different, but the little dragon was insistent. "If we don't stand up to them," he said "they'll think they own the whole Fire Pit." And Amlie had shrugged. It was true after all.

As Guya had predicted, telling his teacher had not meant a permanent end to his problems with Igorr. The Alanas had stopped teasing him at School altogether, but they had started to take other opportunities to play pranks on him when they saw him outside of Fire School. And although it pained him Yoshiko knew deep down that Guya was right. That the only way to stop them was to ignore them. But it would take time.

It didn't help him now, however, as the slow sick feeling crept into his stomach. Even the flash of Alana purple at a distance made his heart race, and a glimpse of Igorr filled him with ugly terror. Yoshiko had felt the fear rising even before they approached the Fire Pit, but as they got closer he knew it was about to happen. He was changing colour. And this time it was even before they had reached the pit. A deep misery sunk through him. He was doomed to be the joke of the whole school. He'd have to take flight again to avoid being noticed. Igorr had repeatedly told many other dragons of his peculiar habit of changing purple after their day flying on the lake and some of the elders had now heard it and had started to make a few whispers about it. So far Yoshiko had managed to hide his colour changing. But even his friends would soon become suspicious if he kept flying away whenever they got close to the Fire Pit. He bit his lip, and began to unfurl his wings when a shout went up.

"Look! I told you! He's changing colour! Yoshiko is turning yellow!"

It was Igorr, but now all the other dragons at the Fire Pit turned to stare.

Yoshiko could feel the colour rising up through him, and for some reason he thought of the sorrel pounding. The deep calm feeling he had every morning as he made the same rhythmic motions, grinding the herbs in the bowl. He couldn't quite put the feeling into words, but it was something about being able to do things for himself, without any help.

For the first time ever, he felt the colour was something he could control himself – as though he'd brought the belief Guya had in him in Cattlewick Cave into the real world. Yoshiko held onto the feeling and knew even without looking that the gold colour was slipping back down, through his feet and away. In the next moment another shout went up.

"Is that what you mean by yellow Igorr? He's red like any other Nephan!" Igorr's friend was laughing at him. "It's just the sun flashing," said another Alana. "You're going colour blind Igorr."

Yoshiko couldn't believe it. It seemed as though he might have learned to control his colour changing.

164

He hoped there would be no other situation where he needed to prove it. But the events had given him a newfound confidence. All he needed to do was think back to the calming pounding of the sorrel, and perhaps the colour changing wouldn't be a problem. He could be normal after all. The young gang of Nephans approached the Fire Pit and this time it was Yoshiko who stepped proudly to the front. "I may not be the best," he joked. "But I need the most practice" and he strode calmly across the outer section. When he came out the other side even some of the older dragons were clapping. Amlie and Elsy were grinning at him.

After that there were only a few times when Yoshiko found his colour rising. Once he was in the Effram hills with Ketu and they had been looking at some incredibly beautiful art. The warm feeling came on and he felt a green colour spreading from his feet. This time he was much quicker, and breathing deeply he let his scales slip back to their normal red before it even crept past his knees. Another time he had found himself frustrated in class, unable to voice what it was he wanted to say, and had looked down to see his claws were as turquoise as a Talana dragon. Quickly he thought back to the sorrel and it slid away. As he learned to control it the colour changing bothered him less, and Yoshiko began to feel almost like a normal dragon. The changing seemed to happen less as well, now that he knew what to do.

It didn't stop him visiting Guya's cave. If anything he knew now more than ever that the making of the sorrel gave him a special calm which helped him in other areas of his life.

He often felt as if he had a secret life with Guya in the cave, and that it gave him a mysterious extra world. It wasn't that he didn't want to share it with his friends, but he was afraid word might leak to the elders who wouldn't understand and would stop the visits. And it was a part of his life he was happy keeping private.

"The dragon was a Nephan shape,
but had no other characteristics that
might give a clue as to who he was.
And then he noticed. The dragon
was made up of different colours.
Every colour of the clans."

Chapter Eleven

Destiny

The morning of boiling the sorrel juice started like any other. Yoshiko rose early, flew to the best sorrel patch, and quickly gathered a bulging net of herbs. Then he travelled to Guya's cave, and troubling the old dragon with nothing more than a respectful nod, got straight to work pounding the sorrel. He had now been travelling to Cattlewick Cave to help Guya for more mornings than he could count, and the work had grown easy with practice. Where it had once taken Yoshiko a long time fumbling with the grinding stone, he now held it with practised ease, making short work of the herbs in the bowl.

Guya no longer came over with extra hands of herbs to add to the bowl, as Yoshiko knew where to find what he needed and had learned the quantities to add. Without even noticing it, he had absorbed almost all of Guya's secret recipe for sorrel juice by heart. But the most important part, the boiling of the herbs, was still a mystery. All he knew was that as he flew from the cave he sometimes caught the scent of the juice bubbling away as Guya worked on it after he left.

But as he went to leave this morning Guya put a gentle hand on his shoulder.

"Do you know the hour of the sun Yoshiko?" he asked. Yoshiko didn't. He thought that slowly, slowly, day by day he seemed to be arriving ever earlier at Fire School. But the time involved was anyone's guess. The hours seemed less important, somehow, when he was in the cave carrying out his work.

"No Guya," he said. "Am I late for Fire School?"

Guya shook his head. "Not at all Yoshiko," he said. "This morning is a good achievement for you. Today is the fastest you have ever made the sorrel herbs ready for the pot."

Yoshiko swallowed, not daring to ask what this might mean.

"Today you may help me boil the herbs," said Guya. "And then we will see what can be done."

Rising excitedly, Yoshiko almost knocked over his bowl, and Guya patted him.

"Not so fast," he said. "Do not get so excited. You have done well to make the herbs faster. But it has taken you several seasons. The next stage is to boil it. This is harder than you think and will take longer. It will be a time again yet before we reach the stage where you are ready to learn the mastery of your own self."

Yoshiko sighed thinking once more how everything with Guya took so long. But he still nursed a secret hope that things might progress faster. If he applied himself and tried hard, surely he would soon perhaps learn some of Guya's secrets and discover more of his

170

own destiny. How hard could it be?

"Pounding the sorrel herbs is easy," said Guya, as if answering his question. "But making the drink itself is hard. Follow me." He led Yoshiko to the dark back of the cave where he had not yet been and pointed out a gleaming copper cauldron. The metal sides shone without stain or blemish.

"First we polish," said Guya. And taking a cloth he began to polish the pot, adding even more glisten to areas that were already shiny. He threw Yoshiko a cloth and gestured that he should help.

"But why do we need the outside to be shiny?" asked Yoshiko. "The sorrel juice goes inside."

Guya's eyes flashed in a returned annoyance. "Always we show the proper respect." He said. "The proper respect for the pot means the proper respect for the process. Nothing is missed out. Everything is important." And he continued his inspection and cleaning of the pot.

"Next collect the water," said Guya. "Over there." Yoshiko saw that in the corner was a simply enormous clay pot. It was almost as big as he was. "Into this pot comes water straight from the sky, through the rock of the cave," explained Guya. "It is special pure water. Good for sorrel juice."

Yoshiko nodded, but he was eyeing the big pot with concern. He had built up some stronger muscles on his arms through pounding the herbs, and he had regarded his new strength with pride. But given the size of this pot he wasn't sure he would even be able to move it. Gritting his teeth he flung his arms around the pot and heaved. It wobbled a little, and some water spilled from the top, but Yoshiko couldn't manage it. Instead he compromised, dragging it along the dirt floor.

Guya looked up at his progress. "No no," he said in panic. "This is an Effram Goadah Pot. Have you never seen one before?"

Yoshiko thought to himself and responded. "No, I haven't, although I have heard of them. Kiara told a story when I was younger, called *The Magic Goadah Pot*. A clever Alana tricked all the Talana clan into saying it could not be lifted."

Guya nodded. "That is just a fairy tale, but they exist in real life too," he said. "The pots are specially made. Very old style, very unique Effram design. Efframs cannot make pots like this nowadays," he added sadly. "This came just after the Surion Battle when the clans were different, and it is very precious. Each clan lost something special Yoshiko, in the years after the Battle of Surion and the longer we have been hidden away in Dragor the worse it has become. The Efframs lost some of their creative energy – they stopped making such incredible things and settled instead on making everyday pots and things from basic clay."

"What did the other clans lose?" Yoshiko had never heard the problems of dragon-kind put this way before. He knew many of the clans became sick as they got older, and they argued amongst themselves. But he always imagined their talents were at their best."

"You have seen for yourself," said Guya. "What happens, for example, when the teacher calls on a Talana dragon to answer a question in class?"

Yoshiko thought about this carefully. "They never answer," he said. "They become shy and upset."

Guya nodded. "They cannot easily communicate, the Talanas," he said. "And what about the Alanas. What do they get into trouble for?"

"Telling stories," said Yoshiko automatically. "Saying things that aren't true."

"Very good," said Guya. "They are not as honest as they should be. But this wasn't a problem the Alana clan was known for before the Battle of Surion. In the legends gone by there is no mention of it. But in Dragor we all well know that Alanas are prone to flights of fancy."

"I became Talana blue," said Yoshiko slowly thinking. "When I felt shy and couldn't think of something to say in class one time. I felt my colour changing and it was blue."

Guya looked at him with interest. "Perhaps this will need more thinking on," he said. "But for now we must make the sorrel juice, and I will show you the trick of the Effram Goadah Pots."

"You must know the right place to hold them and they become very light. Even though they may be full of water as this one is. Here, I will show you." And he heaved himself to his feet. To Yoshiko's surprise instead of putting his arms around the pot Guya moved to it with his back straight, he bent his legs and hoisted the enormous vessel up with ease. Then he set it down again.

"Here, you try," he said. "Keep upright, get close to the pot and use these special places to put your hands. Here." And he pointed out some grips set into the clay that Yoshiko hadn't noticed before. Turning against the pot Yoshiko copied the same position, and found he could now lift it. The task wasn't as easy as Guya made it look, and he still wobbled on his legs as he fought to keep the pot from falling. But, keeping his back as straight as possible he inched over to the cauldron.

"Good," said Guya. "Within perhaps another season or two you will be able to carry the pot easily. Now. I will show you how to tip in the water."

Yoshiko hadn't imagined that anything could be more difficult than pounding the herbs, but it turned out that Guya was right about the boiling process. It was much, much harder. Unlike Kiara, who poured all the water she needed straight into the cauldron, Guya's method involved tipping only a tiny part of water from the giant Goadah Pot into the pan. When it sizzled and boiled away to almost nothing, then it was time for the next few drops. Yoshiko felt his heart sink as Guya showed him the process. It would take forever, he thought.

As he tilted the pot, stirred the herbs, and watched

the water bubble, Guya suddenly tugged at one of his wings.

"Odd shape," he said. "For a Nephan dragon."

Yoshiko nodded in agreement. "When I was younger my elder took me to the Saiga herb doctor dragon," he said. "About my wings, and... the other thing." He still didn't like to readily admit out loud to his colour changing. It made it more real somehow. "The doctor said there was nothing that could be done. I was just born this way. A Nephan who would never be a fast flyer," he added with a snort of disgust. But Guya was shaking his head.

"Nothing wrong with these wings," he said. "But perhaps they do not have the purpose expected of them. When you find out your reason for your wings, then maybe you will not think them so inferior."

"What could they be for?" asked Yoshiko. "Nephans need to be speedy flyers so we can win games."

"But not all the clans win games," said Guya. "What about the Talanas, who need short thick wings to burrow underground easily? Or the Alanas whose big wing span helps them stay in the air a long time?"

"I'm a Nephan," said Yoshiko. "I want to do the things of my clan. Not other dragons."

"Sometimes a dragon is born different because he is an improvement," said Guya. "He has a special purpose." he paused to think. "Do you do much training?" he asked.

Yoshiko looked confused. "Training for what?"

"For flying."

"No." Yoshiko thought about it. He had more or less given up on trying to be a good flyer and flew only when he needed to. He felt he had wings that looked out of proportion for his size, and besides, flying brought back memories of that terrible day on the lake with Igorr, when his skin had turned purple for the first time. "I train to make fire," he added. This was true. Yoshiko had concentrated all his efforts on trying to make big flames to be a Guard like his elder, and though he never expected to be as good as the best dragons at Fire School he was making steady progress.

"You should train to fly," said Guya shortly. "You may find other qualities in your wings besides flying fast and making tricks in the air. Train until you can fly seven times around Dragor. This will be enough practice for you." And he turned back to watch the sorrel juice, letting Yoshiko know the conversation was over.

Yoshiko pondered the matter all the way to Fire School that morning, and again on the way home. Clearly he knew how to fly. But it was also true that once he had learned to get to school and back and travel short distances he didn't bother to improve. As far as he was concerned his short wings had restricted him. Surely, he reasoned, he simply wasn't designed to be a Nephan who won the best prizes in the flying games. What could Guya mean by suggesting he train? And to fly seven times around Dragor? Only the strongest of Guard Dragons could achieve such a thing.

During his work with Guya he had lost a little of his rounded shape, which had been brought on by too many treats from Kiara. Yoshiko knew she wanted to protect him, and food was her way of giving him something extra to make up for the fact that he seemed different from the other younglings. He would never turn away her offerings, they were too delicious, and eating somehow comforted him. But neither did he leave the cave much to fly out with the other dragons.

Perhaps, just perhaps, he thought, if he put more effort into his flying he might find himself leaner and fitter. He might even be able to fly out with Amlie on her long trips around Dragor. Usually he avoided going with her out of embarrassment. He knew he would end up having to take a break while she still had plenty of energy left, and he hated the idea of sweating with effort and gasping for breath. Perhaps it was time for a change.

The opportunity arose that evening when Ketu and Kiara began reminiscing about New Birth's Eve, and their Guard Dragon, Romao. Yoshiko had only met his Guard Dragon a few times, and he knew that Romao always looked on him almost as his own little brother, having been present at the moment of his hatching.

Romao was a very good guard, but he was an even better flyer and expert fire maker. When Yoshiko was younger he had always hoped to be like Romao. But the dreams had begun to slip away as he grew older.

"Do you think Romao would train me?" he asked that dinnertime, interrupting his elders' conversation, and causing them both a moment of surprise. Ketu spoke first, leaning forward to tickle him playfully.

"You little Surion!" he said. "First you spend all your mornings training at the Fire Pit and now you want training from the best Guard Dragon in Dragor! What do you mean by it Yoshiko? I expect you'll be outdoing me at fire and flying soon." He looked delighted at his son's dedication.

Kiara, as usual, looked a little worried. "Are you sure it won't be too much for you to do?" She said. "I wouldn't want you injuring yourself through working too hard."

Ketu turned the warmth of his smile on her. "We shall be nothing but proud of our son," he said. "Of course Romao won't let him injure himself. I'll have a message sent tomorrow." And he put a big spoon of Kiara's fresh sticky mash into his mouth. "My son," he soon continued. "Expert flyer and fire maker. What a proud elder I am." Yoshiko grinned.

Training with Romao was arranged almost immediately, with Ketu keen to set the pair up before his son changed his mind. And before Yoshiko knew it, he was standing in front of the Guard Dragons' cave, watching the large dragons train.

"The secret to flying well is practice, practice, practice," said Romao, as they watched the guards swoop at high speeds over their heads. He heard a similar thing every day from Guya, so he was not surprised that flying seemed to amount to the same thing as sorrel juice.

"Put in the time and you will get your rewards," said Romao. "See these dragons here?" And he pointed to a young dragon, whose scales rippled with the muscle underneath. "He was slower in the air than you when he started," said Romao. "And now he is one of Dragor's best. Every day he trains, around the Trail Mountains."

The Trail Mountains had been specially adapted by teams of Talanas to train the guards. They were the pride and joy of Kinga, leader of the Nephan tribe, who had ordered them to be created so as to allow proper flight training. Since the vast track had been built the flying skills of the guards had improved beyond anyone's highest hopes.

The track used a real mountain range, but the Talana had made some passes much smaller, so that fast flying dragons had to swing almost completely to one side as they flew in order to avoid the jagged rocks. The Great Waters were used so that the dragons could swoop down and hit various check points as they passed over, building up to the perfect score. The flying ability of the guards had become so legendary that dragons now gathered annually for a The Great Race, in which the guards swept around the Trail Mountains to the delighted shouts of the crowds. Yoshiko himself had gasped with delight at the event last season as he watched the guards skim the very surface of the water, smashing the floating pots, purpose built by the Efframs to mark their progress.

"Do you think I could ever fly as well as a guard?" he asked uncertainly. Romao looked him up and down and Yoshiko ducked his head in embarrassment. Clearly a small dragon with clumsy wings would never achieve anything close to the guards' skill, and he blushed a furious red, wishing he hadn't asked.

But Romao didn't appear to be laughing at him. Instead he gave a long slow nod. "Most dragons never practise their flying," he said. "They fly to get around Dragor. But they never push themselves past their limits. If you are willing to train and work hard there is almost no end to what you can achieve."

Yoshiko looked doubtful, but Romao gave another firm nod. "I can see you don't believe me now," he said. "But just wait until we start training. You are young and will see results very quickly.

Finally, thought Yoshiko. Something that can happen fast. But deep down he suspected the training might take longer than Romao was letting on.

"Wing exercises," Romao was saying. "Are the first rule of good flying." He stretched out his large wings and pumped them up and down. Yoshiko watched carefully. He had seen the guards performing these exercises before they flew, and Ketu sometimes did wing exercises outside the cave.

"First we train for strength in the wing," said Romao. "Then we train for accuracy. Come and watch how it's done." And he led Yoshiko into the Guard Dragons' Cave. Inside they were greeted by the sound of clay being smashed and the sight of many more large dragons. They were using their wings to push down hard, breaking thick clay discs as they did so, but the discs were small and a piece of rotating machinery placed them in different places every time.

"The dragon never knows where the disc will be," explained Romao. "They must be fast and accurate as well as strong. Here," and he hefted up a huge thick disc to show to Yoshiko. "See this? One day you will be able to break one of these using only your wing."

Yoshiko turned the disc. It looked impossibly thick. He hoped Romao wouldn't want to try him out on the more difficult exercises straight away.

"Here is where we train to begin with," said Romao. And he led Yoshiko through into a smaller back room. More dragons were gathered, flexing their wings and smashing discs, but they were not as enormous as the others, and to his relief Yoshiko noticed that in this room some of the discs were very thin.

"Good for beginners," said Romao, picking up the thinnest sliver of clay disc and crushing it in his powerful wing. "Very light. And to begin with we will always put the disc in the same place. You have to build up your wing strength before we can progress to accuracy."

He looked apologetic, and Yoshiko decided not to admit that he was relieved they were starting at such a low level. Romao pointed to where he should stand, and he opened his large wings, feeling a flash of discomfort at how out of proportion they must look against all the other dragons.

"Hold them out wide," said Romao, ducking to place the disc beneath the tip of Yoshiko's wing. "Now. Down!"

Yoshiko brought his wing down as fast as he could, and to his satisfaction he felt the thin disc crack under the pressure. "Good," said Romao. "We can try a larger disc." He vanished for a moment before returning with a thicker clay.

Yoshiko's wing thudded into the disc, but this time he only cracked it on the third attempt. Romao looked pleased. "This is the level we'll start at," he said. "Now for the other side."

For the next training they flew out to the red clay hills of the Effram clan where the green dragons were working away on their various creations in clay.

"Why are we here?" asked Yoshiko as they landed. He couldn't think of any reason why they would come to this part of Dragor.

"This is another part of your training," said Romao. "To gain good wing strength and accuracy is one thing.

This will help you to take corners faster and swoop down quicker when you need to. But these skills are only one part of what makes a good flyer. You will need stamina too."

"What is that?"

"Stamina is being able to do something for a long time. It is essential to have this if you are to succeed in staying in the air for a long time. You can be as fast and strong as you like, but to be the best you'll need to keep your strength up over the long term. This is what the winning dragons have – the ones who take the race track right to the end and stay fast and strong."

It makes sense thought Yoshiko.

"A lot of dragons only train for strength," continued Romao. "But if you have both it will help you greatly."

They walked down into the hills, and Yoshiko was still uncertain why they needed to be here for stamina training. They went down towards the Effram's huge clay ovens, as tall as three dragons, and with a fierce flame which could be felt from far away. In front of the oven was a scrawny looking Effram dragon beating the flames with his wings. Romao pointed.

"Do you see that little dragon?"

Yoshiko nodded.

"Don't be fooled by his small size. That dragon has better wing stamina than most in Dragor. Do you know why?"

Yoshiko looked at the green dragon. "He spends all of his time fanning flames?" he guessed. Romao clapped him on the shoulder.

"Exactly! He spends all of his time fanning those flames. All day. Hours and hours. Hardly any dragon uses his wings for that amount of time any more. Those little fan beaters are some of the strongest in all our dragons."

"So what has this got to do with us?" Yoshiko was worried that he already knew what the answer would be.

"We're going to train here as fan beaters," said Romao. "We'll get your stamina up so you can fan flames for hours at a time, and at the end of it all you'll have the best fitness you can achieve."

"Will I be fitter than the other dragons in Fire School?" Yoshiko was thinking back to Igorr, and wondering if he could ever beat him in flying games.

Romao laughed. "Maybe, if you train hard. But it's only yourself you're competing with, to reach your own full potential. Always remember that. You are the only person worth winning against when it comes to training."

"Okey smokey!" he clapped his wings together. "Are you ready to fan the flames?" Yoshiko nodded, looking warily at the little green dragon, who stepped aside at a nod from Romao.

Moving into position Yoshiko opened his wings uncertainly. The green Effram dragon was looking curiously at him.

"That's the way," said Romao. "Now beat them into

the fire." And Yoshiko started to pound his wings together, sending gusts of wind towards the flames. Inside the oven he saw the effect of the air. It tunnelled down under the logs that had been placed in the oven and charged them with a bright red glow.

"The Efframs use air to get extra heat to fire their clay," Romao explained as Yoshiko fanned. "The temperature means their pots and clay works are much harder and tougher. We wouldn't have Effram materials of the quality we do were it not for the fire beaters."

Yoshiko didn't reply, but instead concentrated on the task. He had started quickly, but after only a few minutes he had taken on a more steady rhythm, pushing the air into the flames. It was hard going, and he found a new admiration for the Effram. He had no idea how it was possible to keep up this sort of labour all day. But he pressed on as well as he could. To the side of him Romao seemed to be impressed.

After half an hour Yoshiko was completely exhausted and his wing beats began to slow. Romao, who had been watching him closely, drew him to one side, and gestured that the fire beater could take on his job again. The green dragon moved back into place easily and began beating.

Yoshiko was panting with the effort, but he also felt good. As if some heavy weight had been lifted. It was easy to forget himself in the fire beating.

"That was extremely good," said Romao, who

seemed surprised. He looked up at the sun. "By my estimation you kept that up for a full half an hour. That is the best time I have ever found from a youngling. Have you beaten flames before?"

Yoshiko shook his head.

"Never?" pressed Romao. "Not at home? Ketu doesn't have you fan the fires there?"

"Sometimes for a few minutes," shrugged Yoshiko. "We only have a small fire for one cauldron."

"Incredible," Romao smiled broadly. "You may be behind for speed and turning Yoshiko, but your stamina is already superb. With some training you might even make a Guard Dragon yet." His eyes dropped to Yoshiko's rounded belly. "But one thing at a time. Training depends far more on the will of the dragon than the body. Many dragons start the process and give up just as quickly."

"I won't give up," said Yoshiko quickly. "I'll train every day."

"Maybe not every day Yoshiko, or you really will give up," said Romao. "But every other day would be good. Meet me outside the Fire School at early evening the day after tomorrow and we can train together."

Yoshiko was beaming with delight. So far, he thought, this had to be one of the best days of his life. Romao, whom he had always admired, was impressed with his fitness before he had even done any training. His chest swelled with pride. He vowed to himself that he would train as much as possible and put everything he could into it. Maybe Guya was right about him having a good destiny. Perhaps the training would bring out his talents.

Guya was very pleased with his progress when he reported back to the cave the next morning, breathless with excitement. "Remember Dragor was not made overnight," he cautioned. "Still you must put in good work."

"But Romao said I was the best youngling at fanning the flames he had ever seen!" said Yoshiko. "I'll work hard and soon I'll be one of the best in the training camp, you'll see." But Guya only smiled slightly and ushered him back into the cave.

"Before you master the body you must master the mind," he said, walking him back towards the part of the cave where the sorrel juice was made. "And you know what that means."

Yoshiko sighed. "Grind the sorrel." He said. "Boil the sorrel juice. And one day you'll show me how to drink it properly."

Guya grinned. "You are a fast learner," he said. "Not even ten years and you already know the secrets of life."

Over the next few months Yoshiko worked harder than he had ever done in his life. In the mornings he rose early, gathered herbs, ground them and spent his time filling the cauldron in the way that Guya had instructed. To his delight he noticed differences in his body. His muscles, strengthened by helping Guya, swelled under his scales with the additional strength training with Romao, and he became quicker. His fitness at beating the flames in the Effram Hills became almost legendary in the training school. Local dragons from the clan lined up to watch the Nephan beat flames as well as one of their own dragons, and Yoshiko could now work for a full day in front of the fires if he chose. Neither did he mind this work. There was something soothing about pumping the air forward and continuously, watching the fire drink it up and heat the clay. In those moments he wondered if he should have been born Effram.

He had lost his little belly now, even though Kiara still served him as much sticky mash as she ever did. But somehow it was easier not to eat so much now. The exercise made him feel good, and he was happier.

The only area where he was not doing so well was the strength training. Yoshiko had got better, and moved up several clay discs to a very reasonable level. But he did not seem to get beyond that despite his hours of training, much to Romao's confusion.

"Perhaps your wings are just built that way," he said, with a shake of his head. "Your strength is good now. Good enough, I think, with your stamina to try out for the Guard Dragons when you are old enough."

"But I might never be the most powerful flyer," filled in Yoshiko. And Romao was silent in reply. He did, however, let Yoshiko try for a spin around the training track, racing through the low gorges and narrow mountain passes. They flew together, with Romao taking the lead, and Yoshiko soaring behind him yelping with glee as they zoomed through the chasms and skimmed the low lakes.

"What do you think Yoshiko?" asked Romao. "Would you like to train with the Guard Dragons when you leave school?" And Yoshiko nodded, breathless from their flight.

The next day he arrived at Guya's cave to discover the older dragon was nowhere to be seen. He searched right to the back of the cave, but he was sure it was empty, and a deep dark feeling started in his stomach. Guya, he knew, was very old. What if the dragon had flown off to the graveyard?

With fear rising Yoshiko went for a walk around the edge of the cliff, where he and Guya had first watched the lake. And to his relief he made out the bulk of the older dragon. Guya was seated with his eyes closed, breathing slowly. Yoshiko approached him cautiously.

"Guya?" he said. But no reply came. Worried again, now he drew closer. He could see the dragon was breathing but he seemed to be in another world. Not wanting to disturb him he turned to go back to the cave, deciding to get on with grinding the sorrel and come back when the job was finished. But as he turned around Guya's eyes snapped open.

"Come sit with me Yoshiko," he said.

Yoshiko turned back, and settled himself next to Guya, looking up at him in confusion.

"We have never talked of why I live alone on this mountain," said Guya. "And I am sure you are curious."

Yoshiko didn't answer, not wanting to admit that he had been wondering this every day he had been at the mountain. At school there were always lots of rumours. Some dragons believed that Guya had broken every Commandment of Goadah, but that Kinga had taken pity on him and allowed him to stay in Dragor. Only the worst crimes led to banishment, so it went without saying that Guya must be an evil dragon.

Yoshiko didn't believe any of that now, of course. Having known Guya for several years he thought the dragon seemed incapable of any crime, despite having his oddities and strange ways with words. Yoshiko's own theory was that Guya must have taken himself off into a solitary life. Perhaps something very sad had happened to him. Or maybe he had just decided that he suited this life better, without any other dragons around. It was a strange sort of existence, but if Yoshiko had learned anything from Guya it was that all dragons were different. Even those of the same clan.

"You know Kinga?" he asked.

"Of course." Kinga was the leader of the Nephan clan, and as these dragons were natural rulers of Dragor he was by the same token in charge of making rules for all of Dragor. All of the clans came to Kinga if they had problems, or needed rules to be put in place

190

and he and his council would do their best to solve the issues. He was the most important dragon in Dragor.

"I once sat by Kinga's side in The Council," said Guya. Yoshiko was amazed. He had no idea Guya had once been so important. What could have happened to remove him from such a vital role?

"We were close friends Kinga and I," continued Guya. "We knew each other all through Fire School and respected each other very much. I knew that Kinga would make the best leader, though when I sat with him he was not yet in charge of governing the Nephans."

He stopped as if wondering how to phrase his next remark.

"We made fine rules and saw to it that they were upheld," he said. "And it was very important to me that The Commandments of Goadah were never questioned. We made sure all dragons knew of them. But then one day something happened to change that."

Yoshiko sat further forward curiously. "What?"

"Something happened to me in some distant corner of Dragor. When I was alone, without any other dragon. It made me question The Commandments of Goadah, and eventually I came to look at our rules differently."

"Which rules?" asked Yoshiko.

"Some of the rules which do not permit dragons to leave Dragor and associate with humans," said Guya.

Yoshiko tried not to gasp. Was Guya telling him he had broken the most sacred of The Commandments –

NEVER LEAVE DRAGOR? Secretly Yoshiko had always burned to know what went on outside the mists of The Fire Which Must Never Go Out. But the laws of Dragor were sacred and he had grown up not thinking anyone would question them.

"After that I could no longer sit at Kinga's side," said Guya. "How could I? I no longer believed in everything he stood for. Though I still believed he would become a great ruler and that he would do what was best for the dragons of Dragor."

Guya rocked slightly on his haunches. "I told Kinga I had to go to some lonely spot and make my own path," he said. "Kinga didn't understand and tried to persuade me to stay. We argued. But eventually he saw that I could not be talked around and that I meant to go. That was when he tried to help me. He is still a good friend."

Yoshiko was fascinated. He had never realised Guya had been so close to Kinga. The idea that this lonely dragon had once sat in the most important council in Dragor was incredible.

"I would never tell Kinga what happened to change me," continued Guya. "Only that I knew a different way to protect the dragons of Dragor and must be allowed to do that as best I could. This mountain top is an ancient place of importance, from long ago, in Surion times. Kinga allowed me the spot, and ordered some Talanas to construct it to my needs. He still doesn't know quite what I do up here or why I chose to leave

192

The Council. But he respects me and believes what I do is for the best."

"Will you tell me?" asked Yoshiko. "What happened to change you?"

"No," said Guya simply. "At least not yet. One day I may tell you more of things than any other dragon. But that depends on what path it is that you choose Yoshiko."

Guya looked at him intensely through his clear eyes. "No fate is decided Yoshiko, and you may go one of two paths. Today is the day when you may choose to drink the sorrel juice with me and discover more of who you are, or part my company."

Yoshiko's eyes grew large. Things now seemed to be happening so quickly. Everything with Guya was usually so slow – from the pounding of the herbs for many moons to the back-breaking filling of the cauldron. He realised that he had become quite comfortable with the work, but had stopped expecting the day to come when they would drink the sorrel juice together. His stomach gave a little flip at the thought.

"I wanted you to know this about my past so that you would make the right choice," continued Guya. "I am an outcast dragon. And I believe that in your destiny there is something of the outcast also." He held up a talon at Yoshiko's shocked face.

"Your path is not like mine," he said. "You will not dwell on an empty mountain top. But you have special gifts and this will make your life different from other

193

dragons. You may not want to be different, for it is always a harder road than living like everybody else. You may choose today to drink the sorrel juice with me if you wish. It may answer your difficulties. The question is – are you truly ready to discover yourself?"

Yoshiko thought about this. Over the years that he had met and trained with Guya his life had changed almost completely. He had a confidence about him now that the other dragons at Fire School seemed to sense, and though he knew Igorr and his friends would still take any chance to taunt him, it mattered less. Guya had taught him that it was more important to have a few good friends than worry about being liked by every dragon at school. And every day he felt himself become of less and less interest to Igorr and his friends as he stopped responding to their name-calling.

He could control his colour changing too. And though he was curious to know if the skill actually meant anything, this was the reason he had first accepted the challenge to make the sorrel juice with Guya. He had hoped the old dragon would teach him how to get rid of the problem, but it seemed as though he had done it all by himself. So now that he considered it, he really could become a normal dragon. He could stop coming to Guya's every morning and simply blend in with the others at Fire School.

During his training with Romao he had built up

enough fitness to become a Guard Dragon when he left Fire School – perhaps not the best flamer or the fastest flyer, but a good hard-working recruit nonetheless.

But the more he thought about it the more he realised he had changed. Something was altered now. And it was no longer enough to be like everyone else and pretend he wasn't different. He wanted to know why he changed colour.

Yoshiko knew the path he would choose. "I am ready," he said firmly. "I want to know everything it is you can teach me."

Guya smiled. "I am pleased," he said. "I think you are doing the right thing to discover your true destiny. It may be hard at times, but I believe it is better to live differently and be true to yourself, than to lose who you are trying to fit in with others."

Yoshiko breathed out. The excitement was building now, but something else. Something like fear and excitement combined. Guya got up and beckoned him back to the cave, and Yoshiko followed him through the glittering tunnels nervously. They passed a bubbling cauldron of sorrel juice that Yoshiko had made the day before, and Guya paused to draw out two cups. This was really happening, Yoshiko thought. This was the day he might find out the secret of who he was.

Guya pressed a crystal in the wall and a complicated mechanism whirred, revealing a secret panel that led to another room. Yoshiko looked up in amazement as he entered the secret cave and Guya's flickering candle revealed some of what was on the walls.

It was a mixture of strange symbols and pictures which filled almost every corner of the stone wall. The colours were bright and seemed fresh, but Yoshiko guessed that the images had been in the cave a long time. Perhaps even from before Guya's birth. The dragons shown were different from the shapes of those he knew from the clans. He could see by the colours that here was a Nephan and there was a Talana, but the bodies were a little different from what he knew.

"Did your family paint these?" he asked Guya.

Guya shook his head. "No. No one knows who painted these images," he said. "This hidden cave and the images are from long, long ago. From when the clans settled here after the Battle of Surion. The symbols are a mystery Yoshiko. I have dedicated my life to trying to understand them. But the pictures tell an easier story."

He pointed to a picture in the middle of the cave. Different dragons were painted on the walls, from various clans. Some looked as if they were fighting with one another, and others were running from little figures that Yoshiko guessed must be humans. Still more held spears and looked warlike. But in the centre of it all seemed to be quite an important image and was slightly bigger than any of the others. "Do you recognise this dragon?" he asked. Yoshiko shook his head automatically. The dragon was a Nephan shape, but had no other characteristics that might give a clue as to who he was. And then he noticed. The dragon was made up of different colours. Every colour of the clans.

"It's like me," said Yoshiko suddenly. "A Nephan who changes colour."

Guya nodded. "I think it was foretold that you would come here Yoshiko," he said. "I felt when you first came to this mountain that your arrival was important."

"What does it mean?" asked Yoshiko.

"I don't know," said Guya. "But I did know when you arrived that it was I who must help you if I could. I have seen you learn so much and become wiser from the teachings of hard work and patience. And I am glad you decided to stay and discover more of yourself."

Yoshiko's eyes were following the images on the wall. Part of him didn't believe that the dragon drawn there hundreds of years ago could possibly be him. But something deeper told him that his changing colour was more important than he knew.

Guya was holding out a copper cup filled with sorrel juice.

"You have worked enough now," he said. "To earn the right to drink this sorrel juice here in the sacred cave."

"What will happen when I drink it?" asked Yoshiko.

"You will discover answers," said Guya. "If you are ready for them. You must listen very carefully, very quietly. You must be asleep and yet awake. You must feel as though you are in a trance."

Yoshiko frowned. "How do I do that?"

Guya waved his claw in answer. "You have trained to do it every day Yoshiko," he said. "In the making of the sorrel juice. How do you feel when you gather and grind the herbs every morning?"

Yoshiko paused. "I feel... I don't know. Good about myself I suppose. Confident that I can do things by myself without help." But now that he thought about it that wasn't quite all. There was something else he experienced as he quietly went through the motions of grinding the herbs. As he had become expert, it had become virtually automatic and he almost felt himself slipping into another part of his mind during those early morning hours that helped discipline him in other areas.

"Yes, you feel good about yourself," repeated Guya. "You also feel alert, because you are noticing how the herb is grinding, but relaxed because you have done it many times before and the task is not a challenge for you."

Yoshiko nodded slowly.

"You are well trained in how to listen," said Guya. "I would not have given you the sorrel juice here before because it would have been wasted. Now I hope that together we can find out more about who you are. And what you mean to Dragor."

He handed Yoshiko the cup and raised his own. "Drink Yoshiko," he said. "And we will discover the truth together."

Holding the cup up high as Guya did Yoshiko raised

it to his lips. He drank it slowly, in small measured sips. He remembered the taste from the first time he'd drunk it. It was a special flavour, but it had burned down his throat and inside. This time it was different, it tasted divine. He took another sip.

"Close your eyes Yoshiko," said Guya. "Now. What do you see?"

"I see me," said Yoshiko instantly. The picture had flashed up without his thinking about it.

"And how do you see yourself?"

Yoshiko wrinkled his eyes as if trying to peer deeper beneath the closed lids. "I... I don't know," he said finally. "I just see myself around Dragor trying to find answers."

"Think deeply Yoshiko," said Guya. "Imagine if it didn't matter what anyone else thought of you. No one at Fire School. Not your close friends. Not even your elders. What do you see then?"

Yoshiko frowned. Not even his elders? He'd never thought about himself in that way before. He tried to picture what life would be life if it didn't matter about the dragons at Fire School. Something shifted. In his mind's eye the picture of himself began to radiate different colours in a swirling pattern. He felt a little wary, but there was a gentle wing on his shoulder.

"Don't resist what you feel Yoshiko," said Guya. "It may feel uncomfortable searching, but I am here. No harm will come to you."

Yoshiko relaxed again under the hand, realising how

much he had tensed up. He steadied his breathing, trying to bring back the feelings he felt in his morning preparation of the sorrel, in the same way he did when he was about to change colour.

He had become practised at calling the calmness forward, and it came easier. He breathed again, this time imagining that it didn't matter what Ketu and Kiara thought of the colourful dragon in front of him. His stomach twisted a little. He realised how much it hurt Kiara to think her son was different. Yoshiko nearly snapped his eyes open to dispel the feeling, but once again felt Guya at his side.

Exhaling slowly, Yoshiko allowed the feeling to grow. That it didn't matter what anyone else thought or expected. And to his amazement the Yoshiko-picture in front of him flickered in its pulsing colours and then slowly opened its wings.

He gasped out loud.

"What do you see?" asked Guya.

"The dragon" said Yoshiko. "It's opening its wings. It wants to fly."

"Who wants to fly?" asked Guya.

"Me," said Yoshiko. "I want to fly." He concentrated harder and the wings flapped. Then he saw himself fly high in the sky and Dragor came into the picture beneath him, but far, far away. And he was circling the land.

"I am a traveller," he said finally. "I want to travel the skies." He stopped slightly before admitting to the next truth that came to him. "I want to go beyond the boundaries of Dragor," he said. "But there is something else. I want to do…" he paused. "I am helping the clans. I am dropping some good energy onto them from above."

"What kind of energy?" asked Guya.

"I don't know," said Yoshiko. "But it is raining down on all the dragon clans. And they are happy. They are friends – even those of different clans."

He opened his eyes suddenly, shocked by what he'd just said, and the first thing he saw was Guya's were calming eyes.

"Don't run from yourself Yoshiko," said Guya, sensing that the younger dragon's instinct was to leave the cave. "I want to show you something."

Yoshiko's heart was beating fast now. "But it's not true Guya," he said. "How can I want to break The Commandments, and… and… spread some magic over Dragor? I am not such a special dragon."

Guya said nothing.

"I mean it Guya," said Yoshiko. "What I saw is wrong. I don't want to break the rules, and I don't believe there is something that I can make that can heal the clans. Dragons don't like those who are different from them. That's just the way things are in Dragor."

Silently Guya pointed to another part of the cave that had been dark before. Now his candle cast it in light.

"See this picture?" he said. "It is joined to the first.

You are a chameleon dragon Yoshiko. That is what is special about you. But I did not know what it meant for Dragor for me to find and train you. Any harshness on you was to help you, I knew only that it should be done. And I always puzzled over this picture. But now I know."

Yoshiko blinked as he looked more closely at where Guya was pointing. It was the colourful Nephan dragon again. But this time the picture showed the dragon in flight. And beneath him was a round circle covered in blue and green patterns.

"What is that?" he asked, curiosity making him calmer.

"That is the world," said Guya. "Dragor is only one land, but beyond it are many others. Many, many others. They are not hidden lands like Dragor. And all of them, including our place, rest on this circle that you see. It is actually a globe shape, like a ball. The green is the land, and the blue is something called the ocean. You have never seen an ocean Yoshiko, but it is like The Great Waters that seem to run forever."

"Have you seen the oceans?" asked Yoshiko.

"Yes I have."

Yoshiko sat down heavily. It was the first time that Guya had openly admitted he had broken one the most sacred laws of Dragor. But somehow he didn't feel that Guya was wrong. Instead he found himself desperate to hear more.

"What do they look like?" he said.

Guya smiled. "They can be very calm and very beautiful," he said. "But they can also be angry and dangerous. Everything in Dragor isn't perfect but it is safe. But outside there is both good and bad."

Yoshiko nodded. And then a thought occurred to him. "But what has this got to do with me Guya?" he said.

"Before I answer that question I must tell you a story. Then perhaps you will understand more. Sit Yoshiko. The tale will be a little while in the telling."

Yoshiko sat down obediently, still holding his empty cup from the sorrel juice.

"A long time ago," started Guya. "Long before you were hatched, a young Nephan much like you found a human in Dragor."

Yoshiko started in surprise. Was Guya telling him a real life story? Or was it a fairy tale?

"The human was greatly injured," said Guya. "It was a male human, and the Nephan found him just at the boundaries of our great land. He was dying, Yoshiko, this human. He had somehow scaled all of our defences – our enormous mountains, and the freezing smoke from The Fire Which Must Never Go Out. For you know that the smoke from the Fire is a special kind. It cloaks our land from the eyes of humans who may seek us out, but it also becomes very cold when it reaches the mountain tops. Humankind are not like dragon-kind. They do not have wings or thick scales to warm them. They are soft and their bodies cannot cope with extreme heat or cold. They must keep away from fire."

"Then how did they enslave us?" asked Yoshiko. "If they are so weak?"

"Weak in body is not the same as weak in mind," said Guya. "I hope if I have taught you anything Yoshiko that this is something you have learned. The humans have powerful minds, which they used to trick us all those years ago. They kept dragons drugged with special herbs so that we knew no better than to serve them. And some of them do terrible things to each other and other creatures still. The humans are clever and they are determined. Never underestimate, Yoshiko, the power of one who will never give up."

Guya shook his head a little, realising he'd been distracted from the story, and then continued.

"The Nephan dragon knew that humans were the sworn enemy of dragons," he said. "He knew that the Battle of Surion had been fought to free our kind from them. But still his heart told him that every dragon's duty is to ensure no other creature dies when it can be saved. It was his burden, because The Council of dragons was not as it is now, with Kinga as a kind ruler. It was headed by a less kind dragon, and the Nephan knew that if he took the human to the council they would most likely let him die. And so the Nephan decided to help the human if he could. If it lived, he would try to get it back to the human world. And if it did not he would take the body to The Council and admit what he had found."

Yoshiko listened carefully, wondering what he would have done. He too would have tried to save the life, he decided, even of a dragon enemy.

"The Nephan took the human to a secret empty cave he knew of" said Guya. "And he boiled him up some sorrel juice. Slowly he fed the hot juice to the human, and to his relief it drank a little. Then it opened its eyes and the Nephan could see it was very frightened. The human was very small, Yoshiko, as most humans are. They are shown in our history books as larger, but in fact a human is barely longer than your leg. It had never seen a dragon before in the same way that the Nephan had never seen a human before, and it was terrified to see the huge eyes looking down on it."

"What did it do?" asked Yoshiko.

"The human was too weak to move," said Guya. "And it soon realised that the large creature was trying to help it. So it soon stopped resisting and again began to drink the sorrel juice. And after a while it said something. It said: "This is good.""

"It spoke?"

"Not only did it speak," said Guya. "But it spoke a language the dragon could understand. And what was more, it spoke in the old Nephan dialect. The language that we use for formal council."

Yoshiko was amazed.

"How did it learn the language?" he asked.

"It was the language of its own people," said Guya.

"The Nephan dialect, our dragon language, and this human's language were one and the same. Although perhaps," he added, "with some different words and the way we phrase things here and there. But you would be able to understand this human very well, Yoshiko, if you were to meet him."

Yoshiko hadn't ever thought about humans as being able to speak at all. Instead he saw them in the heat of battle, waving weapons and making war cries, as he had read about at Fire School.

"The Nephan and the human became friends," continued Guya. "As the human got better he was very grateful to the dragon for rescuing him. He wanted to return the favour, and whilst he was recovering he tried to share what knowledge he could with the Nephan. He told him the secrets of special herbs which grow in deep forest areas, and showed him herbs for sickness around the mountain top, those which would heal or grant courage or insight."

"Slowly the human began to explain to the Nephan how he had discovered Dragor. He told him that in the human world he was much like a Bushki dragon clan – he was a man of books and studying. But different also, because he used what he knew to discover secrets of time which were buried in the earth."

"Like what?" asked Yoshiko.

"The human world is much, much older than Dragor," said Guya. "It is where all dragons first came from. And so over all that time many things became buried. Old things, ancient things. They became covered over in the soil. And it is the job of special men to find them and dig them up without damaging them. This man was in charge of finding the bones of old animals which no longer existed."

"Like dragons?"

Guya nodded. "But the human records are such that they no longer know of The Battle of Surion, and the existence of dragons," he said. "Instead they think the dragon bones they find are the same as some other large ancient creatures. They call them dinosaurs. But this man had noticed something. In his digging. He had found a different kind of bones. Ones with wings and special teeth and signs of fire around them, where the others had nothing."

"Dragon bones?" guessed Yoshiko.

"Yes. Dragon bones. And he found many of them in a ring around a set of mountains which no-one could get into."

"So he decided to see what was in the mountains?" asked Yoshiko.

"Yes he wanted to look for himself. And so he climbed the mountains outside Dragor on his own. But he almost died in the attempt, for the smoke from The Fire nearly froze him and the way was very hard. If the Nephan had not found him he would have died and it would have been we dragons wondering what his bones meant," said Guya. "But there was something else," he added, frowning a little. "The dragon bones that he found were not buried alone. They had stones with them."

"Stones?"

"Colourful stones," said Guya. "Special gemstones that glisten and glow. It seemed that the dragons that died outside Dragor had coloured stones buried over the dusts of time with them. And the stones are different for the different clans," he added.

Yoshiko was confused. "What do you mean?"

"The human – he noticed that dragon bones of different shapes chose different stones. And between the two of them the human and the Nephan dragon worked it out. The colours of the clan matched the precious stones which were found in their particular resting places."

"I don't understand," said Yoshiko. "What would the dragons want them for?"

"I know it seems strange," said Guya "but we believe that these dragons knew something they needed outside Dragor, and bought nets of the stones with them from their homelands."

Guya sighed. "Something is missing in Dragor. Something needs to be healed Yoshiko. And I believe it may be that these stones never made it to Dragor. Perhaps the dragons were tricked out of them by the humans. Or maybe carrying them slowed them down or they were forgotten in the horror of battle and bloodshed. The most important thing is," he said "that I believe this destiny involves you. And this picture."

Guya pointed again to the picture on the wall with Yoshiko in flight and the world beneath.

"These are the stones," he said, pointing to where fragments of coloured rock had been pushed into the cave wall to illustrate. "You were born special Yoshiko. I believe you were made to make this journey. To collect the stones back from the human world and return them to Dragor."

Yoshiko's eyes grew wide.

"You have trained long and hard," said Guya. "You have wings that enable you to fly around Dragor seven times, which is more than most other dragons. And I believe your colour changing will help you. The way may be difficult. But it is your destiny to heal the clans."

Yoshiko realised the hand still clutching the sorrel cup was shaking.

"What if I don't want to?" he said in a small voice.

"Then you don't have to," said Guya. "You make your own fate Yoshiko. If you decide this is not your path no one can make you follow it. But if it is, wouldn't you want to find out for sure the mystery of your colours?"

Yoshiko felt the sorrel juice warm in his stomach. The idea grew. That he would be able to leave Dragor. To explore new places. It was a fascinating thought.

"How would I reach the place I need to go?" he said slowly.

"I will help you find a way," said Guya. "But it will be dangerous Yoshiko. You will need all your courage. Go away now, and think about what has been said. Come back when you have decided."

Yoshiko stood to leave, but just before he did a thought occurred to him. "The dragon," he said. "The Nephan who found the human. It was you wasn't it Guya?"

"Yes," said Guya slowly. "It was. And this is the cave where I brought him to recover. He showed me many things Yoshiko. And I am here to tell you that the human world is a beautiful place. Sometimes dangerous, yes. You asked me once before if I thought humans were an evil species. Personally I think they are complicated and themselves spiritually lost though good at heart. They are destroying themselves in their own way. But there are such lovely lands there of the like you have never seen. Sunsets as orange as a Mida, and valleys of green which seemed to go on forever."

It took two full weeks for Yoshiko to decide for sure, but once he did he knew there was no going back. He would go to the human world, and try to help Guya retrieve whatever must be returned to Dragor. Thinking about it made him feel afraid but purposeful at the same time.

Guya welcomed him with open arms, and together they decided on the best plan. Yoshiko would fly out of Dragor, it was ruled. Guya would give him directions to find the human who had once been in this very cave who would help him to return the stones.

"This man has been collecting precious stones for many years," explained Guya. "He knows which are for which clans. He can give them to you."

"Then what do I do?" asked Yoshiko. Guya shrugged. "Bring them back here and try not to get caught coming back into Dragor," he said. "You must spread them into the clans."

This didn't seem like the most straightforward of plans to Yoshiko, but something else seemed to be tugging at him now. Some call of destiny. He felt it every time he entered Guya's cave.

"Take this map," said Guya handing Yoshiko a scroll of parchment. "The human left it to guide any dragons who were worthy of the knowledge to find him in the land of the earth dwellers. It is of no use in Dragor, but outside the smoke of The Fire Which Must Never Go Out you will see the tiny lights in the sky at night-time, much smaller than the moon and the sun so they can't be seen at all through the smoke. You will see the stars. This map will show you how to use them to find the earthdweller."

"When should I leave?" asked Yoshiko?

"This evening" said Guya, "under cover of darkness."

"The voice was not the low whisper of a dragon, but some other sound. He looked around him in confusion and then he saw it. A tiny figure, standing on its hind legs staring up at him."

Chapter Twelve

The Land of the Earthdwellers

Dusk came all too quickly, and Yoshiko looked up. It was a particularly cold night and snow had begun to fall. Guya gave him a warm hug, throwing his arms around him. "Be careful young warrior," he said. "I do not fear for you. I believe it was written that this day would come, and I know it is best."

Yoshiko gulped nervously whilst feeling proud to hear Guya's words. He was feeling more frightened than he thought he would.

Guya pointed to the East of Dragor, far beyond his mountain. "Head for the Burial Ground," he said as he handed him a parchment scroll. "That area is where the veil between the human world and Dragor is the thinnest. The smoke from The Fire is not so cold there, and there are no guards. You should be able to fly up and out without being seen. Use this map."

Launching himself into the sky, Yoshiko swooped through the mountain passes, relishing the chance to put his training into practice in the empty skies. Not knowing what to take with him, he had put a few honey cakes inside his school net and strung it around his wings in case he got hungry, but apart from this he felt light and free. He spotted two Fire Guards making their rounds, and slowed a little, allowing them to pass without seeing him. Then he reached the graveyard without seeing any more guards, and realised his heart was beating out of his chest."

Keep calm, he told himself. He felt the strength in his wings and was pleased with his training. But his mind ached trying to remember Guya's advice.

When you pass the last mountain tops look east. This is where you must go.

He repeated the advice, praying it would be easy to find. He was going to a 'hut' which was a building made only of wood, Guya had told him. This was an odd idea to a dragon, whose world revolved around using wood in the fires.

Taking a deep breath Yoshiko wheeled and flew straight up much higher into the sky, steeper than he had ever flown. As he gained height the fear grew. He was about to break one of the sacred Commandments of Goadah – NEVER FLY ABOVE SURION MOUNTAIN. Then another feeling swelled inside of him. The excitement of being where no other dragon had been, of discovering a new place. *I am made to do this*, thought Yoshiko filled with so many emotions.

Up at the mountain tops the smoke from The Fire Which Must Never Go Out burned at his eyes and he coughed. It grew very cold and he shivered beneath

214

his scales. But still he flapped his wings and went on ever higher. Then he saw it – the top of the mountain – and his heart leapt.

Yoshiko was growing more tired now, and his wing grazed the top of the rocks as he flew up and over the mountain, but still he went. For a moment he felt sad, he wished Guya had been with him to share this experience. The Fire Which Must Never Go Out kept them all in a comforting fug of smoke. But here the night was fresh and new, and he could see a hundred lights in the sky. They were the most beautiful sight he had ever seen, and Yoshiko stared up at them. He unfurled the map and looked up. The lights matched marks on the paper, and he found he could easily follow them, and flew onwards. Leaning to the right he tracked the stars until they stopped as he was flying over the middle of a snowy mountain.

He landed on the cold ground, and took another moment to stare up at the incredible lights above his head. Then to his shock he heard a voice.

"They are amazing aren't they? You don't have them in Dragor. But we earthdwellers see them every night."

Yoshiko opened and shut his mouth, not knowing what to say. The voice was not the low whisper of a dragon, but some other sound. He looked around him in confusion and then he saw it. A tiny figure, standing on its hind legs staring up at him.

"Are you a human?" The words were out before he

could stop himself.

The little creature made a sound which could have been a laugh. "Yes I am," he said. "And you are a dragon. A Nephan if I am not mistaken. I know from your red colour. And a young one, I think, by your soft scales."

"I am Yoshiko of the Nephan clan," said Yoshiko formally. "I have come to find the Keeper of the Stones."

"Well then Yoshiko," said the human. "You may call me the Keeper of the Stones if you wish. But I would prefer that you called me Gopal. That is my proper name."

"Gopal?" Yoshiko tried it out, rolling the unfamiliar name around in his mouth. He liked it, he decided. Though he had never heard such a strange name before.

"Come," said Gopal. "Follow me. Guya told me you would come one day."

"How did you know I would come tonight?"

Gopal pointed at the sky. "It is written there," he said.

Yoshiko stared up at the sky. "You can read the lights?" he asked, impressed. Gopal inclined his head but didn't answer directly. "I come out here every night to watch as the sun sets," he said. "And so I knew one night I would find you."

Gopal began to walk back down the snowy slope, and Yoshiko went slowly after him, confused by the strange human. In the far distance he could still see the Surion mountain.

"You can see the smoke from our mountain from a great distance." Yoshiko remarked.

"Yes," said Gopal. "It is called the Dragon Mountain by people in this part of the world due to the smoke that bellows. Little do they know that dragons actually live there."

"We must live in secret of course" Yoshiko exclaimed. "The volcano is what won us The Battle of Surion and created Dragor to keep us safe."

"Of course, I hadn't forgotten about the eruption," said Gopal. "Guya told me, your land was sealed when the rocks and lava began to fall. It was this very mountain with a heart of strong fire that burst open when Surion was slain. It may look different to you here in the land of the earthdwellers, because here it is covered in snow on the lower parts. That is unusual in the human world. Volcanoes are more often found in hot places. Bubbling hot rock boils inside it and sends up smoke, and sometimes, very rarely, it bursts open and sends flaming liquid down its sides. But that hasn't happened since Goadah's mighty roar. We humans have our own similar story about that mountain that we consider a fairy tale," he added. "We believe that there is the heart of a dragon in its centre, and the beating heart keeps the local people safe from harm. That is why we call it Dragon Mountain."

By now they had reached the lower part of the slope,

and there was a soft light in the snow. On the horizon was a cave, but not like one he had ever seen in Dragor. This cave was barely big enough to fit an adult dragon, let alone a family.

As they got closer Yoshiko could see that the little cave was actually built from the wood of trees.

"This is my home," said Gopal. "Not like the caves you live in. Much smaller than you are used to, but then we earthdwellers feel the cold more strongly than dragons and so we heat smaller spaces with our fires."

So this is the hut that Guya spoke about and humans did have fire after all, thought Yoshiko. He could see it glowing brightly inside. And smoke poured from a little chimney. He had learned at Fire School that only dragons could make it.

They reached the door and the human opened it to reveal a small room made entirely of wood. Yoshiko had never seen anything like it. There was a little brass stove that kept the room cosy and warm, and a small comfortable looking bed. The only other objects were large chests that were lined up against the wall.

"I know why you have come," continued Gopal. "Maybe better than you do. I have been studying your kind for many years, and I believe that you dragons left something behind after the Battle of Surion. Something that you need back for the health of your clans. Your charms."

Yoshiko didn't know how to answer. The human already seemed to know his mission.

"I have been collecting stones for you," said the human with a little smile. "But I do not keep them here." And taking up a large key from a closed drawer he beckoned Yoshiko back outside into the snow.

They walked on into the distance and soon a much larger building came into view. This time, Yoshiko noted with satisfaction, it was made from stone. But unlike the rocky caves of Dragor which were carved from mountains, this one stood alone. It had the most perfectly straight sides on the bottom, but rose into many steep roofs stacked one on top of the other. Yoshiko was amazed.

"It is called a pagoda, this shape," explained Gopal. "It is also known as a temple. This is where people come to be healed."

"Why do the humans need to be healed in a temple?" Yoshiko had assumed that the earthdwellers already had all they needed from medicins and herbs.

"The dragon clans learned all their darkness from men when they lived as slaves to us," said Gopal. "Humans have much spiritual healing to do, and not all of us work to learn it. But the more informed people do, and they come to places like this to be taught." He swept his hand up towards the building in front of them.

As they approached Yoshiko had a calming feeling. As if all of his problems were melting away, and there was nothing but contentment ahead. And the nearer to the hut they came the stronger he felt it.

"It is the call of your stones," said Gopal. "Do you feel it?" Yoshiko nodded.

The doors to the temple were much larger than Yoshiko, and this time he could easily follow the human inside. Once they were past the doors Gopal lit a candle, and the incredible contents of the temple were revealed.

Wide metal bowls contained stacks of bright colourful gemstones, glittering in the glow of the candle. Every colour of the rainbow was represented, and Yoshiko felt his eyes grow wide as he saw them. Deep inside he knew that the rocks had a good purpose for Dragor. Next to them was a metal frame made into a tree shape. Its silver branches had hundreds of the multi-coloured stones hanging from them with tiny metal clips, which he realised must be what Gopal referred to as charms.

"I am many things as an earthdweller," said Gopal, noticing Yoshiko's reaction to the stones. "I found Dragor because I made it my life's work to study the bones of animals buried in the ground. But in doing so I learned a lot about different human races as well as the clans of the dragons. I am a healer now," he said. "People come to me because I understand what different stones can do to help them. They bring me gifts," he added. "Everyone who comes to be healed by my knowledge brings me a stone. And over the years they have grown into this collection which you see here."

Yoshiko had heard about the many different precious stones in stories, and some dragons had them and treasured them but he had only ever seen a few in his life. And here the abundance of them in all their bright colours shone out. He could feel their power and the energy.

"What is it I am feeling?" asked Yoshiko.

Gopal let out a long breath as if wondering how to explain. Then he sat down and gestured for Yoshiko to do likewise.

"I am not as wise as our wise friend Guya," he began. "But I do know something of Dragor and the dragons. And there is something in your history which you were not told."

Yoshiko looked at him in amazement. How could this human know anything about Dragor that he didn't?

"The battle between the humans and the dragons happened long, long ago," began Gopal. "Long before my lifetime, and that of almost all the dragons."

Yoshiko thought back to The Ageless Ones and wondered if they really did live back to the Battle of Surion.

"The dragon clans hatched in the many mountains of the earth. The female dragons crushed and ate the powder of certain rocks to help form the egg shell and their young," explained Gopal. "These mountains were from a wider more extreme environment than where humans lived and contained many different stones. Some of these are very rare, and all formed from

221

special minerals, and as the earth moved it shifted some of the oldest powers into the stones."

Gopal paused to check Yoshiko was still listening.

"The dragons have many special powers, but to be at their best they all need the special stones of their homelands around them. The mountains where the different clans were made have special powers which the dragons need. That is why you will find in Dragor there is discontent and unhappiness. The dragons feel they are missing something. But they don't know what. That is why sickness affects your dragons, and the clans quarrel and fight one another."

"Can we ever come back to our mountains?" asked Yoshiko. But Gopal shook his head.

"These places are ruled by humans now," he said. "There is no room for the dragons. But there is a solution of sorts to the problem."

"What is that?" asked Yoshiko.

"Bringing the stones to the dragons of course," said Gopal. "What you are here to do."

"What will happen?" asked Yoshiko. "If I bring the stones to the clans? Will all the problems be over?" He thought of the many sick dragons in the herb doctor's cave, and the fighting amongst the clans.

But Gopal shook his head.

"There will be problems in Dragor whilst the clans battle with one another," he said. "At the moment there is nothing you can do about that. But the stones will help heal and bring greater happiness. Once they have been scattered the dragons will regain their true powers and feel healthier in their bodies."

"All the clans have a different stone," added Gopal. "The Nephans have the ruby stone. This is what you are feeling when you are in this temple. The peace of being so near the stone of your birth mountain. Many of these ruby stones can also be found in the mountains near where we are," said Gopal. "I believe that is why Surion chose to make your homes in Dragor. Not just for the protection of the mountains, but because he wanted to be near the stone of his clan."

Yoshiko found himself walking towards the pile of red stones.

"That is your rightful stone," said Gopal.

Yoshiko felt the power of the stones inside the chest soak up into him. "It seems to give me energy and a feeling of confidence," he said.

"Good" said Gopal. "I know from Guya that you dragons could benefit from having your correct stones back." He gestured towards the first pile of stones, a deep blue in colour.

"These are sapphires" Gopal explained. "This dark blue stone helps with intuition."

"What's that?" asked Yoshiko, moving towards the glowing stones.

"Intuition is a knowledge of your inner feelings," said Gopal. "It is when you know something is true from deep inside you."

Yoshiko started. He had known that he had a special

purpose for Dragor, but until he'd met Guya he had never dared to think it could be true.

"The sapphire expands your dreams," continued Gopal. "It helps open your mind to consider the magic outside your own world, it attracts blessings."

Yoshiko thought back to the blue Saiga dragons of Dragor. It was true that they were the most spiritual of the dragons. The Ageless Ones were Saiga and they seemed to have the gift of intuition which Gopal talked of. But the clan also seemed to be often frustrated and lacking in courage. Could the sapphire stones help heal them? He remembered back to his conversation with Guya, when the old dragon explained how the different clans had problems which were not recorded before the Battle of Surion.

"These are amazonites," said Gopal, moving now to a pile of turquoise stones. "They help communication."

Once again Yoshiko called to mind the clan which matched the colour, and saw how the stone seemed to fit. The blue Talanas were well known for having problems talking with the other clans, and were shy and withdrawn. If what Gopal said about the stones was true then the amazonite stones would be the perfect fit to help the Talanas overcome this problem.

"What are these?" asked Yoshiko, pointing to the piles of vibrant green and deep yellow stones.

"These are green jade and yellow citrine quartz," said Gopal. "The first encourages a sense of belonging, creation and more effectiveness. It could help your

Efframs make the incredible pots they have long given up making," he added. "And this quartz will help lift any sadness and anxieties that the Bushki has."

Yoshiko remembered what Guya had said about the Goadah pot he used to make sorrel juice in his cave – how Efframs no longer made such fine items. Then he pictured the nervous Bushki dragons looking calm and confident. He smiled at the thought.

"Can you guess what these are for?"

Gopal was pointing to the last two piles of stones, one orange and the other dark purple. Yoshiko thought carefully.

"Well the Midas could do with being kind on themselves and happy, they often worry" he said, pointing to the orange stones and imagining the agricultural clan who tended to hate any idea of change, and were known for being hard on themselves over the slightest mistake.

Gopal nodded. "Very good. Those are called sunstones. They are good to boost self worth. And these?" he was standing by the last pile of stones.

"Being kind to others?" Yoshiko was thinking of Igorr and the Alana Clan.

Gopal nodded his head, but he was smiling. "Yes, in a way they do Yoshiko. They are amethysts. This stone makes people more wise, gives them self-control, and calms harsh emotions."

Yoshiko thought about Igorr, who seemed unable to stop telling lies.

Gopal was looking at all the stones now, and back at Yoshiko.

"I spent a lot of time thinking about how you will carry them and also how the other dragons could carry them at all times," he said. "So I decided to turn them into charms, like little pendants that could be worn around the neck and I have prepared all these on this metal frame."

Yoshiko looked at the charms glistening. It was the most magical tree you could believe. He had seen trees adorned by the dragon clans at their winter time celebrations but nothing compared to this. And then something occurred to him. The scales on his wings. The ones the doctor had said should perhaps have been clipped back by now. These were just perfect to hang the charms from.

Curiously he unfurled his left wing. "Could you..." he looked at Gopal. "Will they hook here?"

Gopal leaned underneath the wing and clapped his hands together delightedly. "Why then!" he said. "Your wings have grown scales the perfect shape to hold these charms. It's as if you were made for them."

Gopal filled the underside of both of Yoshiko's wings with the first charms, and there was just enough room for all of the jade green ones. They jingled under his wings, chiming together in their own music.

"You will have to make a different trip for each colour," said Gopal uncertainly.

Yoshiko thought back to his training with Guya and realised why the old dragon had told him to work up his strength to fly around Dragor seven times. He must have known that Yoshiko would be called upon to deliver the stones in this way.

"I have been practising," he said slowly. "I think I will be able to make the journeys."

"Then this is how it will be Yoshiko," said Gopal. "You must deliver these green ones quickly, and when you have finished come back here and I will give you the next colour. We must finish by dawn."

Yoshiko nodded. With the charms draped around him he noticed a pulsating feeling of contentment, as if anything could be achieved. "I hope to return quickly."

Launching back into the night sky Yoshiko headed away from the stars and back towards the smoky skies of Dragor. As he flew the stones around his body moved in a happy sound, like a hundred little bells. It was a soothing noise and he let it ring into the night sky as he flew back towards Dragor, with the charms sparkling in the moonlight.

Although he'd only been gone a few hours Yoshiko felt as if he were a completely different dragon. He'd seen things no other creature in Dragor except Guya had seen. He also knew if anyone found out he would be in big trouble – but he had an immediate problem. Now he had the charms how could he drop them? He realised he had to stay high in the sky to avoid being seen by the guards in the light of the Dragor fires. He must fly above the smoke, but this meant he was too far away to know where to drop his load of charms. The jade charms must be scattered in the Effram clan lands, this much he knew. The stones started to grow heavy on his body as he hovered around wondering what to do.

Then suddenly Yoshiko could feel a familiar sensation, a colour change was happening and by the light of the moon he could see that he was turning a bright green. He realised he must be above the Effram clan, his body had sensed it. The colour changing was there to allow him to drop the stones on the clan from a great height. Whilst he couldn't see with his eyes where the different places of the dragons began and ended, the colours of his body were telling him how to drop the stones in the right places.

Smiling to himself Yoshiko fluttered his wings very quickly and the bright green stones fell from his scales, down over the Effram area.

The first charms were gone, and Yoshiko wheeled in the sky, heading back to the land of the earthdwellers. Gopal was waiting for him, and had already laid out the next batch – the deep indigo charms of the Saiga clan.

"Are you sure you can make it?" he asked Yoshiko. "All the charms must be dropped tonight."

Yoshiko shook his head. "I'm not in the least bit tired," he said, as the blue sapphires were loaded onto his wings.

Yoshiko repeated the process for the Alana and the Mida clans. After the fifth journey, and then the sixth, where the yellow and blue stones were dropped on the Bushki and Talana clans, his wings had grown tired. He could hardly lift them but still he summoned all his strength one last more to collect the charms of his own clan from Gopal, the red rubies.

"Take care Yoshiko," said Gopal, who could see how exhausted the dragon was. "I know you will deliver these last charms. It is your destiny." And he waved with both arms as Yoshiko launched into the sky for the last time, leaving the land of the earthdwellers far behind him.

Yoshiko had dropped all of the charms over Dragor, and though he was sleepy he felt utterly content. It was as though a part of him had finally been fulfilled, and he flew back to Dragor, not home, but to Guya's cave. He knew Ketu and Kiara wouldn't be awake for another few hours, and he wanted to talk with the old dragon about the events of the night.

As he landed on the deserted mountain he saw Guya was waiting for him outside the cave. He handed him a cup of steaming sorrel juice.

"I did it, Guya," said Yoshiko, his eyes gleaming like the stars he had seen. "I went to the human world. I met with the earthdweller there, and he showed me the stones that he had turned into charms as a gift to the clans. And somehow I knew what I had to do. I flew above Dragor and I dropped them over the clans. My colour changing helped me. Guya, do you think this is what I was destined to do?"

Guya nodded. "I do Yoshiko. I think your gift of colour changing came to grant the dragons peace. After The Battle of Surion, Yoshiko, it was a time of great sadness as well as celebration. Our great leader Goadah's son died in battle and many of Dragor's Commandments were made during a time of great uncertainty."

"I believe that we dragons are in touch with more magical powers than we realise," he continued, "and in times of trouble we call on it to bring us special dragons, chosen ones to help our cause. It happened with Surion, from the red egg, and it happened with you. At the time of your hatching there was much talk about the egg from which you were hatched. No dragon knows what happened to the shell, apart from perhaps your elders. And so it was decided by The Council not to take any action to record things any differently. I suspect Ketu or Kiara, like any caring elders, did not want their hatchling to be seen as different, and so somehow the shell was hidden."

He stared out into the night, sipping on his sorrel juice. Yoshiko thought about this. He had seen in Amlie's cave that her elders kept the shell from which she had hatched and displayed it proudly. The question suddenly occurred to him, why had his elders not done the same thing? Thoughts now whizzed through his mind, Ketu's tale of the wicker basket, the over-protectiveness of his Mother, his colour changes. Could he have come from a special egg like Surion himself?

"It is time for you to go Yoshiko," said Guya. "You have done well tonight, and we will see tomorrow the effect your bravery will have on the clans."

Yoshiko nodded, suddenly feeling very tired. The sun had not yet risen on the horizon, but he could tell it was very close. He leaned in and gave Guya a brief hug, and then he took off back into the night sky.

When he got back to his cave Ketu and Kiara were sleeping peacefully. Yoshiko crept to his perch and fell fast asleep.

The night was one the dragons would talk about for years to come. Many swore they heard above them a jingling in the sky, like the ringing of a hundred bells as they perched sleepily in their caves. Then as they woke they found colourful stones had been scattered throughout their clans. The dragons raced out excitedly to discover their world was covered in bright charms, which lay on the blanket of snow like a fallen rainbow, and gave each of them a special feeling of peace and power. They gathered them up and took them back to their caves, resolving to celebrate this special day with the other clans.

Yoshiko awoke to see Ketu's eyes level with his own.

"Wake up Yoshiko!" he said. "You've overslept. Not surprising considering all the hours you've been putting in at the Fire Pit. But you must come down at once. Something has happened."

Yoshiko unhooked his claws and let himself fall back down to the ground of the cave.

"What?" he said, wondering for a moment if perhaps something had gone wrong. Part of him had expected to wake up to find the events of the previous night had all been a dream, and at the very least his scattered stones would raise some curiosity and nothing else.

But Ketu led him to the mouth of the cave and picked up a ruby-red stone from the entrance. "Do you feel it?" he said, holding the stone close to Yoshiko. "It is a charm. All the dragons have them this morning. Something happened in the night, and we have had magic delivered to us, and... Can you feel it Yoshiko? The power of it? I feel whole again. As if something that was missing has been found."

Kiara joined them at the entrance of the cave, a blissful smile on her face. The line of worry which Yoshiko often saw on her forehead was gone completely. "It is a beautiful day Yoshiko," she said. "Some miracle has come to the clans. The spirit of Goadah has come and left gifts for us all."

They were interrupted by the sudden arrival of Romao. He skidded to a halt outside their cave entrance. "You have your charm?" he said. "I have flown over all of Dragor. All the clans have them, but they each have different colours. Here we Nephans have red, but the charms are different for all the dragons."

"Do all the other clans feel it?" asked Ketu.

"Yes," said Romao. "All have woken to know this is a special day, with gifts from the Spirit of Goadah delivered to us all. Kinga has called a special council to decide how we may celebrate."

Ketu and Kiara looked at one another excitedly. "A feast day!" said Ketu. "That is what he will decide. Let's start making up the sticky mash now."

Suddenly a great fanfare went up.

"It is the Guard Dragon," said Ketu. "They are calling loud enough to be heard all over Dragor. Kinga must already be calling all the clans to The Council." The family looked at one another. "We must go and hear what is being said," said Ketu. "Perhaps Kinga knows the source of these incredible stones."

As they took to the skies Yoshiko and his elders joined the throngs of other dragons from all over Dragor who had been summoned by the call. And even though the air was far more crowded than usual, no dragons were flapping impatiently or trying to overtake the slower dragons. Instead they all flew happily, and smiling at one another. Many of them had hung the charms around their necks. Yoshiko felt a secret inward burst of pride knowing he had done this and that he held an incredible secret.

They landed at the Council circle, and Kinga was standing on his haunches greeting the dragons one by one as they landed. Soon clans from all over Dragor were settled, and Kinga picked up a carved horn to make his voice loud enough for everyone to hear him.

"Welcome to The Council, citizens of Dragor!" he announced. "I am honoured that so many of you could be here today, and I think we all know the reason for this meeting."

A ripple of agreement went around the assembled clans.

"Last night, while we all slept, a great blessing came to Dragor," said Kinga. "Charms fell from the sky. They sought out the different colours of the clans, and brought to us a peace which we have been missing. All of those who feel the special power of these charms raise your claws."

The air was thick, suddenly, with talons raised aloft in agreement.

"We must be sure to give thanks to Goadah for this gift," said Kinga. "But we also must discover if there is another part to the puzzle. If any dragon knows of how these charms came to be delivered, speak up and we will hear it."

There was silence amongst the dragons. Every one of them was filled with curiousity.

"Then it is a gift from Goadah himself," said Kinga. "And we must decide now how we can give thanks for it, and make this day special."

But suddenly a croaky voice went up from the midst of the crowd.

"Wait Kinga," called an old female dragon. "I know of how these stones came to arrive. And when you hear of it you will not be so pleased to have these evil charms in your clans."

Kinga's face showed shock and he peered around for the voice. And then he saw her. Yula, the old Hudrah, in the middle of the dragons.

"What do you know of it Yula?" asked Kinga. "Can you tell us how these gifts came to arrive?"

"Not gifts," said Yula, and as the crowd turned to look it became obvious that she was the only dragon without a stone.

"You cannot call them gifts, for they do not come from a dragon world."

The dragons began to talk amongst themselves. Not all of them could hear Yula, whose voice could not carry as Kinga's did, and many were clamouring to know what it was she was saying. Others who had heard her were whispering about what she could mean. Could it be that the charms were evil from outside Dragor?

Yula began to make her halting walk through the crowd to the centre of The Council, and the crowd parted to let her through. She reached Kinga, and bowed her head respectfully.

"Ten winters ago a dragon was born to this clan who I warned the council about," she said, her voice husky. "Surely many of you here must remember that a certain pair of elders present were granted a strange egg?"

The whispers started again. Could Yoshiko have something to do with the charms?

"I warned The Council," repeated Yula. "I even tried to take the hatchling away before it could do harm for Dragor. But I was stopped by this Guard Dragon," she pointed accusingly at Romao. "But I knew that one day Ketu and Kiara's son would bring a curse to Dragor, and I followed his elder when she hid the evidence of his strange egg." From inside her cloak Yula pulled out a bundle of cloth which she held aloft triumphantly.

"See here," she said. "I have the pieces of the shell which Kiara and Ketu would have hidden from you all. See where their youngling Yoshiko came from!"

And she opened the bundle to let the shining fragments of shell fall onto the ground. As the shell dropped, the glittering colours shone in the rising morning sun, and the dragons saw them in all their glory. Several nearest to the shell pieces moved away for fear of touching them accidentally, and gasps went up as the crowd looking at the abnormal shell.

"What does this mean for Dragor?" shouted a Talana, enjoying her newfound ability to communicate. "If Surion's red egg brought disaster for the dragons, then this coloured shell must be worse!"

"Wait," said Yula, eyeing the Talana harshly. "I have not yet told all. I have watched this hatchling as he has grown, for I always knew something was wrong with him. And over the years I have seen him for what he is. He changes colour!" And she pointed an accusing finger through the dragons directly at Yoshiko.

As all the clans turned to look towards him, Yoshiko thought that his usual techniques could not save him now. But he fought with every part of his body, and slowly sent the rising colour back down through his feet and into the earth.

Then another voice went up.

"It's true," Gandar was shouting over the dragons. "I have seen it. My son and I, we both know he changes colour. It is not right." Igorr was standing next to him, nodding in agreement.

"But it is worse than that," continued Yula. "This strange dragon broke The Commandment of Goadah last night. I saw him. He flew up past the furthest mountains of Dragor and he vanished for many hours. He was visiting the forbidden world – the world of the earthdwellers!"

This was too much for the assembled dragons, and they all broke into excited shouting and talking. For a dragon to break the rules was unthinkable. Such a thing had never happened in their history, and there was no real knowledge even of how to punish such a crime. And for a youngling at that. Many did not believe it.

A great roar went up and everyone was silent suddenly. Kinga had spoken.

"Come forward Yoshiko," he said, gesturing to the centre of The Council.

With every nerve trembling Yoshiko made the slow walk through the dragons. He was terrified. But worse was the knowledge that his elders would know he had hidden the truth from them. Slowly he approached Kinga, who bent down to whisper into his ear.

"Well young Yoshiko," he said, with a glint in his eye. "Something tells me this has something to do with wise old Guya."

Yoshiko was too frightened to reply.

"I cannot save you from the suspicions of the clans," he continued, "for Dragor's different dragons will love the chance to prove a Nephan has broken the rules. But I may be able to find a solution if you are brave enough to take a test." He frowned as though he was thinking of an answer to the problem, and then he raised the great horn to address the crowd again.

"I have examined the youngling," he said loudly. "And there is no way his wings could be powerful enough to leave Dragor and break The Commandments. But the question of his shell is a serious matter. I decree that he should be tested in the ways of Goadah. Yula is a great Hudrah for the Nephans, and does her best to protect the clans, and we must listen to her wisdom. But even she may sometimes be mistaken. The pieces she thinks to be shell could be no more than a colourful Effram pot."

He raised his spear. "But all dragons must be given a

fair trial," he continued. "And so Yoshiko will be given a chance to prove himself. He will watch over The Fire Which Must Never Go Out. And if he guards Dragor successfully for one night then it is Goadah's will that he is not a cursed dragon."

He looked sternly out onto the dragons, as if daring anyone to disagree with him. Guarding The Fire was usually given as an honour to older dragons, no youngling had ever been placed in this position. Yoshiko bit his lip nervously.

"If he does this then hear no more about strange shells and strange dragons," said Kinga. "However, we must not forget that Goadah looks favourably upon us in the bringing of these stones." He paused. "And so today will be a day of great feasting whilst we enjoy the power these charms bring us."

The crowd began to cheer. A feasting day was always appreciated in Dragor. They seemed a little less concerned about Yoshiko's suspicious hatching now that Kinga had set the test. Yoshiko tried to calm his nerves. He was being granted the duty of a full-grown Guard Dragon and he knew he must fulfil it. After circling Dragor dropping charms at night, guarding The Fire would be easy, or so he thought.

Kinga gestured that Yoshiko should return to his elders in the crowd. He reached Ketu and Kiara.

"Why didn't you tell me?" he asked, looking at Kiara. "About my shell?"

"I... We didn't want you to think you were different,"

said Kiara. There were tears in her eyes. "Because they might have taken you away from me."

"But I am different," said Yoshiko. "My scales change colour."

"The doctor said it was something you'd grow out of," she said, but she looked uncertain.

Yoshiko shook his head. "It is part of who I am. I wanted to hide it, and to make you proud of me, and be like the other dragons. But I'm different from them. And that's why I didn't tell you about my visits to Guya,"

"You're not different Yoshiko," said Kiara, but Ketu stopped her.

"Of course you're different," Ketu said. "Every dragon is unique. I don't know about what Yula said to you Yoshiko. About whether you broke The Commandments. If you say you didn't I believe you. Neither do I fear for you with this test. You are old enough to guard The Fire properly, and the faith of the dragons will be restored. You will earn a great honour."

Yoshiko nodded twice to his father respectfully. Keeping his visits with Guya hidden had been difficult. He wished he could tell them the truth of his journey to the land of the earthdwellers. But he felt for now that at least part of his gift must be kept secret.

"We must go and gather sorrel for the feasting day," said Ketu brightly. "We'll go now before the other dragons get there."

The family took to the skies, while still many eyes

on the ground were on Yoshiko as he flew up with his elders. They gathered the sorrel, and for Yoshiko it felt strange to be with his elders having made this journey every morning alone. But he was enjoying working with other dragons as they rooted up the leaves of the bushes.

"You've got much faster at gathering sorrel," commented Ketu as Yoshiko's practised claws took up the leaves. There was a little flash of understanding in his eye, as if he knew there were things unsaid.

The rest of the day was dedicated to feasting and celebration as promised, and all the clans gathered to tell tales of what the charms had done for them, and share food together. Huge bowls of fruit and sticky mash were prepared along with limestone pies, honey cakes, and enormous cauldrons of sorrel juice. There were fire displays from the various clans, and a flight of Guard Dragon took to the air to show their skills.

At the end of it all Yoshiko and his elders flew home bursting with the day's food, but unlike the others they weren't as happy from their holiday. They knew Yoshiko must still be tested. As they flew back towards their cave this time they passed over the market place from where Guya's mountain top could just be seen, and Yoshiko had a sudden pain to imagine his friend alone when all the other dragons were feasting. He looked across to see that Guya was out of his cave, waving happily at him in the distance.

"You have fulfilled only part
of your destiny Yoshiko," they said.
"The delivering of the charms is only
some of what is needed
to heal Dragor."

Chapter Thirteen

The Fire Which Must Never Go Out

"Guarding The Fire Which Must Never Go Out is the very highest honour in Dragor," said Romao firmly as if Yoshiko didn't know already. "Although I understand that you are given this role in slightly different circumstances I have no doubt, Yoshiko, that you will take that honour seriously."

Yoshiko nodded. He had been with Romao for four hours now, learning the various important duties of guarding The Fire. The privilege was usually reserved for guards who had performed exceptional service, and Romao himself was often granted the duty. It was hard work. Dragons appointed had to constantly stoke The Fire overnight, without sleeping even for a moment. Special fragrant logs were used by night, which burned with a perfume smell, covering Dragor in the scent through the night and helping the dragons to have happy dreams. But this kind of wood burned more quickly to produce more smoke than the daytime kind, and needed far more attention to keep it alight.

The Fire Guard dragon also had to wear a heavy headdress for the ceremony, which for a youngling like

Yoshiko was oversized and very uncomfortable.

"You'll get used to it," said Romao uncertainly as he heaved the weight of feathers and stones onto Yoshiko's snout and fastened the strap under his chin. Wobbling a little Yoshiko turned his head experimentally. It would be very hard, he decided, to carry out the duties when he was so much smaller than the dragons who usually earned the honour.

Romao had found a way to make the headdress slightly less cumbersome by tightening the strap that wound around his tail, and Yoshiko moved a little more easily.

"It is important you can move well," said Romao. "You will need to bend very low and blow air into the flames."

He demonstrated, throwing himself flat on his stomach so that his nose was level with the very lowest part of the flames.

"Blow a very steady stream of air," he explained. "Don't puff into the fire or you will cause it to jump and make sparks. But don't be too weak either. A strong steady breath." And he blew out a stream of air right into the bottom of the fire.

The logs glowed with a fierce red colour as he blew on them, and then the fire above puffed up into proud high flames.

Romao got back up off the floor. "Like that," he said. "Now you try."

They spent the evening practising and training, and

not for the first time Yoshiko was struck by what a good teacher Romao was. It was easy to learn from a dragon who was patient and never treated any question as if it was wrong. The job was not easy, but as they practised he found many of his worries slipping away. Yoshiko felt more confident he could pass the test and guard The Fire properly for the clans.

As dusk fell Romao gave Yoshiko a respectful bow of goodbye before turning to launch into the sky.

"You are the Guard Dragon with the honour of guarding The Fire Which Must Never Go Out," he said formally. "May the flames rise high through the night and the dragons and Dragor sleep peacefully."

Then he leaned forward whispered. "Good luck Yoshiko. You'll do a fine job." And away he flew.

Left all alone Yoshiko surveyed The Fire with a practised eye. And though it didn't really need it he bent down and blew a stream of air into the flame as Romao had taught him. His heart soared with pride as the flame leapt, and he took a moment to enjoy being guardian.

Then from somewhere in the darkening distance he heard the sound of claws scraping the ground and a dragon landing.

He blinked into the darkness. Perhaps Amlie or Elsy had come to talk to him. He knew it wasn't allowed, but he would be glad to see them, he thought.

But to his shock from the mist of the rising smoke a purple dragon appeared. It was Igorr. Yoshiko tried not to show his surprise.

"What brings you to The Fire Igorr?" he asked.

Igorr gave him a slow smile. It looked strange on his face in the flickering light of The Fire. "I've come to apologise to you Yoshiko," he said.

"Apologise?" Yoshiko was instantly suspicious. Since he had begun his training, relations with Igorr and his gang were less difficult, but they certainly weren't friends. And Igorr had been only too happy to side with Yula when she tried to expose his colour changing.

Igorr sat down. "I know I've treated you badly Yoshiko," he said. "But from now on I would like us to get on better. I have brought you some of Agna's sticky mash as a present." And from a net somewhere on his back he brought forward a bowl of mash wrapped in a purple cloth.

Yoshiko wasn't sure what to do. He didn't like to reject Igorr's gift when the Alana dragon was finally being civil. Reaching forward he took the bowl, ducking his head in gratitude.

"Thank you Igorr," he said carefully. "I would like us to get along better. Perhaps you would do me the honour of sharing this mash with me?"

But Igorr shook his head. "Keep the bowl," he said roughly. "My elder won't mind. I'll see you at Fire School." And he took off suddenly, leaving Yoshiko wondering if perhaps he'd dreamed the other dragon's arrival.

Sitting down he unwrapped the cloth and took a small taste. It was particularly sweet, and he gulped it down gratefully. There was another flavour too. Something he didn't recognise. It must be some special Alana spice, he thought.

Yoshiko went back to guarding his fire, but all of a sudden he began to feel strange. His eyelids were dropping. He dragged them open but without his being able to help it they began to close again. Panicking he tried to stand but something in his legs felt too heavy to move. What was happening? He'd only been guarding an hour and he was feeling as tired as if it were the middle of the night.

Concentrating on the flames Yoshiko's head was spinning. He rolled heavily to one side, unable to control his movements and the headdress slipped down over one eye. Then Yoshiko fell with a thud to the floor, and into a deep, deep sleep.

Before he knew it he was dreaming, and he saw himself floating up into the sky and towards a dark deserted mountain. Unlike Guya's mountain this one seemed strange and dark, and Yoshiko was drawn towards a set of caves where he landed.

There was a noise behind him and he turned in alarm to see the strange clanking sound belonged to three enormous dragons. Unlike the flesh and scales of Dragor's inhabitants, these creatures were made from metal, and moved slowly towards him, blinking with unseeing eyes. Yoshiko turned and ran towards the shelter of one of the caves.

Inside the walls were dripping with green slime, and little red eyes winked out at him. Yoshiko was petrified and yet something drew him forwards towards whatever creatures lived in this cave.

A horrible shrieking rose up, like knives over rock, and a huge winged bat flew out suddenly, crashing into Yoshiko's face. It had grubby white fur, with a blunted nose and long yellowed teeth. As Yoshiko tried to fend it away another came, and then another. Before he knew it he was covered in evil bats biting and scratching at him. He fell down under the weight of them and a pair of red eyes appeared level with his own. Then the fanged mouth opened up and a hissing sound came out – *Yoshiiiko*.

Picking himself up he turned and ran through the cave, and as he did a tiny chink of light came into focus, which became larger as he got nearer. There were huge spiders now joining the bats chasing him through the dark, and for a moment Yoshiko thought there was no way out. Then he realised the growing light was a crack in the rock, just big enough for him to squeeze through. Gasping for breath Yoshiko pushed through it to great relief, leaving the nightmare horde of bats and spiders behind.

Outside the cave was as different from inside as night was from day. It was a world of beautiful green valleys, of rolling sunlight brighter than he had ever seen, and a lovely blue sky. Taking flight Yoshiko soared above, drinking in the colours and the scenery.

And then suddenly someone was calling his name.

He awoke to shouting. Romao, he thought he could hear. And Kinga. Lots of running about and flames jumping. Yoshiko opened his eyes groggily, dazed and confused. He wasn't at home on his perch, but on a rough earth floor.

Then he remembered. The Fire. There was a sick feeling in his stomach.

He pulled himself unsteadily to his feet and found himself face to face with an angry looking Romao.

"The Fire Which Must Never Go Out!" he said. "What were you thinking Yoshiko? Falling asleep?"

Yoshiko didn't know how to reply. He had no idea what had happened.

Kinga drew alongside him, looking serious.

"Luckily Romao was keeping an eye on things," he said. "He saw that the Fire was about to go out. The Great Fire, Yoshiko! Do you know what this would have meant for the clans if it had been allowed to burn out? All of Dragor would have been exposed to humans! Our way of life as we know it would have been in danger. I thought you would complete this test, but you have failed me."

Yoshiko hung his head dumbly. There was no

excuse, he thought, other than the tiredness had come on so quickly he hadn't really understood it.

"All the dragon clans will soon know of what has happened, some will have seen that the smoke veil thinned and nearly disappeared," continued Kinga. "And your crime is a very great one Yoshiko." Kinga looked sad. "For many dragons this will be evidence of truth about the coloured pieces which Yula claimed to be your shell. They will think you do not respect Dragor's laws. You are to be put in prison Yoshiko, until I make a decision about what to do."

Yoshiko felt the light flood out of his world. Yes, Dragor had a prison of sorts, but it was a relic. In his lifetime no dragons had ever been placed there. It acted more as a warning to uphold The Commandments of Goadah.

"It must be done," said Kinga. "This is a very uncertain time for Dragor. No-one knows where the stones came from or how they arrived. And though the dragons feel their benefit many will wonder if the stones will have bad effects as well as good. They suspect you may be involved somehow."

Yoshiko was speechless, and to his horror it was Romao who arrived at his side to lead him away.

"I know you made a mistake Yoshiko," said Romao. "I don't believe anything that the dragons have said about you bringing a curse. But it is my duty to take you to the prison. I am sorry."

Yoshiko bowed his head. There was nothing left to

say.

They didn't fly to the prison, but instead made the long walk past where The Council met on the rocky outcrop behind. Romao pointed and Yoshiko trooped ahead. There was only one cell in the prison – Dragor had never needed more – and Romao had tears in his eyes as he slid the rock door into place. A small hole had been carved through the thick stone to allow Yoshiko to look out but, apart from the tiny shaft of light coming through, inside was completely dark.

Romao walked away, and a new guard moved forward to take his place guarding the gaol. Yoshiko felt total despair wash over him, and as he watched his entire body began to take on this time the darkest red colour. He was too depressed even to bother to push the colour away to his bright red shade, and instead let it envelop him.

Yoshiko sat down to consider his situation. He was in utter disgrace, and despite fulfilling his destiny and delivering the charms to the dragons he was now locked away. A great tear rolled down his cheek as he imagined Kiara and Ketu hearing the news of his imprisonment. He tried to work out if they would visit him or if they would be too ashamed to come to see their son in prison. He decided they probably would come to see him, but he would rather they didn't.

There was a tap at the rock face and a guard's face appeared at the door. He looked alarmed. "There is someone to see you," he said.

Yoshiko look shocked. He had been there just minutes, how could anyone know he was here already? A wave of shame swept over him. Could the gossip have spread so quickly, maybe the dragons at Fire School had come to shout taunts.

"I don't know how they know you are here," said the guard, apparently thinking the same thing as Yoshiko. "Under Kinga's orders no one has yet been told of your imprisonment Yoshiko. But you have two visitors."

The guard stepped away and at the little window appeared two entirely blank faces. It was The Ageless Ones.

The two dragonesses had left their usual spot at the market place and somehow made it down to the prison. No one had ever known them to move beyond their own clan or their market spot, so it was perhaps no wonder that the guard was so confused. Yoshiko could just make him out hovering in the background trying to hear if The Ageless Ones would break their legendary silence and actually say something to him.

The two heads turned to look at the guard, and he quickly stepped away before their empty gaze as if understanding they wanted privacy. Then they leaned back in towards the window, so only Yoshiko could hear them. Before he could ask anything of them the twins began to speak at the same time.

"You have fulfilled only part of your destiny Yoshiko," they said. "The delivering of the charms is only some of what is needed to heal Dragor."

Yoshiko was silent in shock to hear them speak and in such eerie and ancient tones. Yoshiko knew Dragor was divided as to whether these two old dragons held ageless wisdom, or were simple-minded. But Ramao had told him once how Ketu believed The Ageless Ones knew things about Dragor from long ago, and that they quietly watched over the clans.

"The charms help the dragon clans balance themselves," continued one of the twins. "Dragons are not like any other creatures. They do not live only on sun and air, but also need the energy of the rocks of the earth that you have returned to my sister and me. Before now great knowledge was lost."

They stopped as if remembering something sad, and then carried on in unison. "In his grief Goadah wanted to keep the dragons safe, and he ignored what they had left behind. But the time has come Yoshiko, for Dragor to be reunited with the last of what they have lost."

Yoshiko was confused. "But I delivered the charms."

"There is something else," said The Ageless Ones. "You gave the dragons the stones for each clan. But there is another stone. A special stone. This is the final stone to heal the clans."

"A special stone?" Yoshiko was confused. "Where?"

"You must go again to the land of the earthdwellers," said the dragonesses.

Yoshiko's face tightened in anger. "The last time

I did that I ended up here," he said. "I'm not going to break any more rules. I'm tired of being told it's my destiny. Guya should have warned me this would happen. He should have seen it."

The Ageless Ones shook their heads. "Guya doesn't know everything Yoshiko," they said. "He has been chosen to guide you, to help you. But after that you must choose your own path. No dragon can live your life for you."

"No well-intentioned dragon should end up in prison!" said Yoshiko. "Even if I wanted to go back to the land of the earthdwellers I am stuck in here and there is no way out."

The two blank faces blinked at him, but gave no indication that his words had any effect.

"It is your destiny Yoshiko," they said. "Go and find the rose sapphire. Heal the clans."

And then as suddenly as they arrived they were gone. Yoshiko stared out from the little window. The twins had vanished.

He sat back down on the cold floor of the cell, feeling totally confused. Why did it have to be his destiny to help Dragor? It wasn't as though any of the dragons were grateful. They had shut him up in prison. But the truth was the idea of returning to the land of the earthdwellers appealed to him in some whispering kind of way. It was an incredible land outside Dragor. He could still picture the lights in the dark sky, stretching out endlessly, and the cool fresh breeze around his wings.

Yoshiko shook his head trying to dispel the image. He was in enough trouble as it was, without breaking the rules again. The Council had already put him in prison. Who knows what they would do if he was discovered returning to the human world. Perhaps he would even be banished to some remote Dragor corner, never allowed to see a dragon again.

Then again, he reasoned, the last time he had brought the stones, the dragons had been happy at first, when they felt their effect. Perhaps this special new stone would have a stronger impact. Maybe they would forgive him everything and would understand that his birth wasn't a curse to Dragor. Unable to make up his mind he got to his feet and walked back to the door of his cell. The guard was nowhere to be seen. It was as if he had vanished.

Then, as Yoshiko watched, the door of his cell creaked open. He started back in alarm, wondering who was coming into the prison, but as he stepped forward towards the open door he saw that there was no-one there.

He moved out of the cell cautiously, thinking of how he could explain the events to the guard if he came across him. Perhaps it would be better to return to his cell and wait it out with the door open. But something made him walk on. Had The Ageless Ones done something to the prison? It was impossible to tell. But all he knew for the time being was that if he chose to be, he was free from his cell.

Different thoughts rocked through him. Escaping from the prison could hardly make matters better for him. But then again they couldn't be much worse. Something brave took hold of him and remembering all his training Yoshiko made his decision. He would return to the land of the earthdwellers and take his chances. Better to take the risk and know for certain than stay forever in Dragor wondering if his destiny would have been different. He spread his wings and took to the air.

The journey was easier this time and as Dragor became small beneath him Yoshiko breathed in the clear air as he rose over the smoke of The Fire Which Must Never Go Out. It was daytime this time when he landed, and instead of the black sky with its white lights he saw a blue colour stretching up above. Then as he drew lower the dark mountains he had seen on his past visit were green valleys beneath him, with bright sunshine lighting them.

He blinked as he flew lower. He couldn't believe it. It was the land from his dreams.

After he had been chased by the bats and spiders he had escaped to a place which he thought only existed in his imagination. And here it was. The human world was beautiful, just as Guya had described.

Exhausted with the events of the day Yoshiko settled on the ground to regain his strength. As he did so doubt seized him, despite the scenery before him. Here he was far away from his homeland. For a second he wondered if he would be allowed back, perhaps the Guard Dragons would be sent to protect Dragor to stop his return, he thought, and let him be killed by some evil humans. The human land seemed very lonely suddenly. What if he was stuck here forever?

Then he looked up. Tracing the outline of the sky above was a beautiful bow of colour in a great arc across the sky. It painted every shade of the clans, from the blue Saiga clan through to the bright red of his own Nephan clan.

A peaceful feeling stole over him. He remembered the seven charms, each picked out in the colour of the clans. "A rainbow of seven colours," he said out loud, thinking back to some of the storybooks of dragons before the Battle of Surion. Rainbows were not seen in Dragor, but in the human world they were a sign of hope. Perhaps it was a sign he was on the right path. He felt his worries float up into the sky, and picked himself up to continue his journey.

He had to find the earthdweller himself this time, and landing on the patch where he had first met Gopal he recalled the path to the little wooden hut, wondering how he would be greeted. The door was flung open before he had the chance to tap on it and Gopal's face lit up with a wide smile to see him.

"So you have come again Yoshiko," he said. "Welcome back."

Yoshiko couldn't help but smile in return. It felt as though it was the only friend he now had.

"I was unsure about coming back," he admitted. "But I have been told there is another stone. A rose sapphire. It is needed to heal the dragon clans. All is not yet well in Dragor," he added.

Gopal's face set more seriously. "I think I know what it is you're looking for," he said. "Come inside."

Once they had crossed into the hut, Gopal took up a chair, and sat down. "It is a difficult thing you ask for," he said. "And I am frightened for you Yoshiko. When you came for the first stones it was an easy thing for you to deliver them with my help. But this stone you now ask about... it is something different."

Yoshiko tried not to let his fear show on his face. What if he could not return the stone to the clans? He would be an outcast.

"I never thought it would be something the dragons needed," continued Gopal. He pointed up towards the smoking mountain in the distance. "Do you remember the story of the dragon's heart in the volcano?"

Yoshiko nodded.

"I didn't tell you everything I knew about that story," said Gopal. "They say that long, long ago a dragon was seen entering that mountain. It came out a broken and sad creature." Gopal paused.

"It is said in this part of the world that it is a real

dragon's heart which beats in the mountain."

Yoshiko's mind was racing as Gopal continued.

"No man could get through the scorching heat to find out for sure of course but I believe there is some truth to this legend," said Gopal "and Surion's heart is in the mountain."

"What do you mean?" asked Yoshiko.

Gopal shook his head. "Whilst of course a dragon's heart couldn't really beat there. I believe that Surion may have put a special stone in that volcano, for safe keeping. A special stone that has in it all of Surion's love for the clans. I believe he left there the stone of unity – a rose sapphire. Pink like the colour of love and with many special powers. I believe the stone you need is in the volcano. In the heart of the flames."

Yoshiko felt his stomach twist. A stone in the heart of hot boiling liquid. He thought back to the Fire Pit and tried to fight down the rising feeling of panic.

"I can't do it Gopal," he blurted. "I can't go into the volcano. I am the worst of all at the Fire Pit." Images of Igorr's taunting face were swimming in front of him.

Gopal's face was pulled into a patient smile. "Well I can't go in there," he said. "The fire would burn me to a cinder before I even got close." he eyed Yoshiko critically. "You have the softer scales of a younger dragon, but the strongest will of all. I think you could get through the heat or The Ageless Ones would not have sent you."

"I don't know," said Yoshiko quietly. "People think I

can do many things and –"

"– And they are right" interrupted Gopal. "Guya asked you to come to the land of the earthdwellers to find me, and this you did. He showed you the picture of you dropping charms on Dragor, and this you did. What has anyone thought you capable of which could not be done?"

Yoshiko thought about it. Gopal was right he had achieved a lot but he failed to stay awake at The Fire Which Must Never Go Out. And walking through flames was something different. The fear rose up again.

"What if I can't do it?" he said.

Gopal shrugged. "Then you can't do it," he said. "The question you should be asking is how will you feel if you don't try?"

Yoshiko tried to picture it, and he knew Gopal held wisdom like Guya. Maybe he could get the rose sapphire and maybe he couldn't. But he couldn't go back to Dragor without trying to bring the stone that could heal the clans. He took a deep breath.

"Will you take me to it?" he asked Gopal. The man smiled. "I think it is you who will take me," he said. "We earthdwellers can't fly so well. But if you'll let me travel on your back we can get there very quickly."

It felt very strange taking to the air with a human on his back, and Yoshiko flew extra carefully so as to keep Gopal comfortable. He landed at the foot of the volcano but Gopal gestured he should fly higher, to the smoking top. Yoshiko could feel the heat as they got closer, and as he touched down on the rocky earth he saw that Gopal was sweating.

"The heart of the volcano is down there," he said, pointing. "I cannot go any closer Yoshiko. But you must journey down through the flames. If the stone is in there it will be on the other side of the hottest part, held safe from men."

Below them was a liquid fire, boiling and belching up thick plumes of smoke. It churned angrily, as if daring anyone to approach it, swirling in orange and red.

Yoshiko was in the grip of a strong fear and unable to reply, he simply ducked his head at Gopal, flew down inside, and began to make his way into the depths. Dry and hot rocks skidded beneath his feet, but he soon reached the far edge of the molten centre. It rolled out like a dark river in front of him.

Carefully he let one of his feet sink into the boiling liquid. It closed smoothly over his talons and Yoshiko felt the first wave of strong heat rise up into him. It was hotter than anything inside Dragor, even at the hottest part of the largest Fire Pit. Steeling himself he took another step, trying not to gasp. And then slowly, slowly, he drew himself forward until his belly and then his shoulders were fully immersed.

Beneath him the liquid was deep and Yoshiko realised he would not be able to wade through without letting his head sink under. Instead he would have to swim. The fire was coursing through every part of him now, and he could feel his soft scales beating in pain. Trying to keep his breathing steady in the heat as he had been taught to do, Yoshiko brought up his wings in the lava and began to swim through the liquid fire, copying the way the Alana dragons moved when they swum with their heads above water to catch fish too small for their nets. The heat was so intense he thought he might faint, and every single inch on his body was screaming. Sweat dripped into his eyes so that he was almost blinded, and combined with the smoke belching up he could hardly see where he was going.

Come on Yoshiko, he found himself saying in his own head. *You can do this. You are brave and strong.* He spoke again out loud, trying to convince himself further, affirming to himself. Then Yoshiko thought back to Dragor, and how he could ever return without the stone to heal the clans. With a determined kick of his legs he powered forward. He had to keep going.

After what felt like a lifetime Yoshiko reached the far side of the volcano, and through the haze he could just make out a little dark patch in the rock. To his relief he found he was able to pull himself out of the terrible lava and onto a rocky ledge.

Yoshiko let the heat leave his scales, and looked around wondering what to do next. It was then that he felt a totally unknown sensation. A calm feeling that seemed to beat through the whole inside of him. And he knew he must be close. Out of the corner of his eye he saw a flash of pink against the red and orange of the rock, and headed towards it.

As the smoke cleared Yoshiko saw the most beautiful stone glistening. He let out a quick gasp at how stunning it was. It was shaped almost like a heart, and had been set into a part of the rock face. It was a soft and delicate pink almost the colour of a newborn hatchling. As he drew closer Yoshiko felt the pain from his scales drop away and a feeling of deep love sweep over him. He used his claws to pull it out from its setting in the stone and held it up in amazement.

"Let's see what you can do for Dragor," mumbled Yoshiko to himself as he looked at the stone, and he could have sworn it winked back at him in the light of the flames.

The way out of the volcano seemed much easier than the way in, and Yoshiko felt as though holding the stone gave him some extra protection from the heat. I will never fear the Fire Pit again he thought bravely, as he flew back to where Gopal was waiting for him at the top of the volcano.

Yoshiko returned Gopal back to his hut, and they waved to each other with a greater sadness this time and Yoshiko headed back to Dragor wondering if it would be the last time they met. If the rose sapphire didn't work then the chances were he thought at best that he would be thrown back in prison whilst the clans decided what to do with him.

As he flew up into the sky, and back into the mists of Dragor, however, Yoshiko did have a quiet feeling that everything was going to work out for the best. Although he didn't know if it was the rose sapphire that was making him feel this way, or something else.

His homeland came into view, and Yoshiko realised he was glad to be back in the world of the dragons.

There was a sudden gust of air at his side and Yoshiko turned in shock to see The Ageless Ones had taken to the sky and were flying alongside him.

"Follow us Yoshiko," they said, turning in the breeze. "We will show you where to put the rose sapphire stone." And so he followed them, wondering if he was the only dragon to have ever seen them fly.

They flew over The Great Waters and the two dragons stopped suddenly, beating their wings to keep them in the air. Yoshiko wondered what was happening. There was only water beneath them.

"Where are we going?" he asked. But the twins pointed down in reply.

"Drop the stone Yoshiko," they said.

"Drop the stone?" Yoshiko couldn't believe what he was hearing. "But I've taken it back from the land of the earthdwellers. It needs to go somewhere where it can help the clans."

"The rose sapphire is a stone of love Yoshiko," said The Ageless Ones. "It doesn't take its power from fire or air. You must drop the stone here for it to release its full power."

Looking down Yoshiko understood what they meant. The Ageless Ones wanted him to let the stone fall into The Great Waters.

"But it will be lost!" he said helplessly, thinking of the deep waters below them. Not even an Alana could hope to retrieve the stone from those depths.

"You must trust the power of the stone," said The Ageless Ones. "Ask it. Feel it. It wants to help Dragor."

Yoshiko's wings were beginning to tire. But something in him felt a little tug from the stone. As if it sensed the water below. Another part of him wanted to hold onto the stone. To prove to the other dragons that he'd taken it from the volcano. That he'd been a hero.

"Let it go Yoshiko," repeated The Ageless Ones. "You will have your glory another time."

And digging for one last burst of strength, Yoshiko surrendered to the stone and let it fall, far, far below, until it hit The Great Waters and sank without a trace.

For a split second Yoshiko felt a wave of endless sadness, as he thought he had done the wrong thing.

And then, like a burst of warmth, The Great Waters shone pink in an endless beautiful glow, and a light began to rise up.

"You have saved Dragor Yoshiko," said The Ageless Ones. "You have united the clans in love and understanding." They turned suddenly, and were gone as quickly as they had arrived.

Yoshiko flew back to his cave, feeling the power of the rose sapphire as it swept over Dragor. He knew finally that he had done the right thing. If all went well Yoshiko would go to Guya later and they would drink sorrel juice, and celebrate. But now he needed to explain to Ketu and Kiara.

Yoshiko's heart sank as he approached the cave. Outside the entrance was The Council Spear. Kinga was visiting Yoshiko's elders. Letting his talons scrape the rock as he landed, Yoshiko braved himself for what was to come.

Inside he heard the voices not just of Ketu, Kiara and Kinga, but also of Yula. *What was she doing here?* Wondered Yoshiko, thinking back to Yula's speech at The Council. Probably she had come to spread more gossip.

But the voices sounded happy, and his first sight of the dragons was of them sitting drinking sorrel juice and smiling contentedly.

Kinga was the first to see Yoshiko, and he looked up with his eyes full of admiration.

"Come, our hero" he said. "I have come from The Council to make an official apology to you."

Yoshiko's mouth fell open in shock.

"Yes, yes," said Kinga. "Yula here came to us with some information. It seems that she knows something of Igorr's mother Agna, and the strong sleeping herbs she takes."

Yoshiko looked on in confusion.

"I hear that Igorr paid you a visit with some sticky mash," continued Kinga. "Yula saw it all and found the mash pot after you'd eaten. It seems that Igorr put some of his mother's special sleeping herbs in it. That was why you fell asleep on duty Yoshiko. It wasn't your fault."

Yoshiko looked to Yula then Kinga and back again. He could hardly believe that Yula had come forward with this information.

"Yula only wants what is right for the clans," said Kinga, noticing his expression. Yula looked down in embarrassment, but Kiara reached forward and patted her arm.

"Have some more sorrel juice Yula," Kiara said. "We are all very grateful to you. If it wasn't for your sharp eyes Yoshiko would be back in prison."

Yoshiko gulped, wondering how he would explain the escape, but once again it seemed Kinga had a story ready.

"The guard on duty told us that The Ageless Ones insisted he let you leave the cell," he said. "And of course these wise dragons were right to do so. Perhaps a little over eager," he said with a twinkle in his eye. "But right nonetheless. Now Yoshiko," added Kinga. "I must talk with you alone, with permission of your elders." He looked at Ketu and Kiara who nodded, and gestured that Yoshiko should follow him outside the cave.

It was a beautiful evening in Dragor, and Kinga allowed himself an enormous smile as he looked out over the land.

"Something special is in the air," he said. "I don't know what it is. Some great contentment. But I think all the dragons feel it." he turned to Yoshiko with a smile. "I don't know if I have you to thank for it Yoshiko," he said. "But I am sure my friend Guya will explain some of it to me – if not everything." He grinned as if this didn't matter to him.

"But I do have something serious to talk with you about, Yoshiko," he said. "All is well with the clans, and we have much to celebrate. I am anxious because for any dragon to leave Dragor is against The Commandments of Goadah. And these cannot be broken. Even in special circumstances."

Yoshiko dropped his head guiltily.

"You must promise me Yoshiko," said Kinga. "By the sacred Commandments of Goadah, that you will uphold the laws of Dragor, and never again venture beyond our boundaries."

Yoshiko hadn't thought beyond what would happen once he had returned to Dragor but finally replied "I have no reason to leave Dragor."

Kinga seemed to accept this as his agreement. "Good," he said. "I feel that you have done great things for Dragor, Yoshiko. Perhaps things that I will never know of. But that time is past now, and you must celebrate along with the rest of us. I am declaring another feast day tomorrow in honour of the clans, and I also expect to see you take part in the next Fire Games."

Yoshiko breathed out. The prospect of taking part with the other younglings had taken up all of his attention during the first year of Fire School. But in his training with Guya it had somehow become less important to win awards for the games.

"I'll enter the Fire Pit event" he said, remembering his promise never again to fear it after the volcano.

"I'm sure your elders will be very proud," said Kinga. "Now Yoshiko. Come back into the cave and we'll finish up Kiara's sorrel juice. We all have much to be grateful for."

"No youngling has ever been able to endure that heat," he announced. "And Yoshiko has gone further even than the older dragons. So for this game he has earned the highest honour - the Fire Spear!"

Chapter Fourteen

Yoshiko's Glory

Yoshiko stood at the entrance of the Fire Pit, and ignored Igorr, who stood beside him as a fellow contestant, at last without taunting him. Since Yula had made it public that Yoshiko had been given sleepy herbs by him even Igorr's close friends had seemed to drift away from him, and no one held him in high esteem. Nevertheless, his skills with fire meant he had been entered to represent his clan in the Fire Games.

But even Yoshiko's friends Amlie, Elsy and Cindina had been anxious about him taking on the Fire Pit so publicly. It was New Birth's Eve and whilst the dragons with eggs were hidden away in their caves, all the rest of the clans were out to celebrate with feasts, and the favourite Fire Games of the year.

"Are you sure you want to do this Yoshiko?" said Amlie. "You haven't had any time to practise, and this is the hottest the Fire Pit has been all year."

She didn't mention that both she and Elsy had seen Yoshiko fly away from the Fire Pit before, but the unspoken words hung in the air.

Yoshiko thought back to the volcano, and gave them both a wide grin. "It's nothing," he said. "I can do it. There are hotter places than this one."

Amlie and Elsy dared not smile back, but wished him luck, and continued to watch him anxiously as he drew nearer the pit.

A youngling from every clan had been selected to be the first of the year to take on the outer parts of the biggest Fire Pit, which had been stoked especially for the competition – far stronger than its usual training temperature. Ayo and his Fire Guard had been heaping up fuel and blowing huge lungfuls of air into the flames all morning, heating the inside of the pit red hot.

After the younglings' attempts the older dragons would step forward for the proper competition, where they would try out the deepest depths of the Fire Pit for the greatest honour of the day, The Flaming Spear.

Yoshiko had volunteered to try out for the Nephans, and although his fellow Fire School dragons weren't keen for him to compete Kinga had ensured his place. He felt only confidence as he saw the dragons older than him also line up against him.

The roar of the Guard Dragon went up and the younglings began to venture forward into the flames, one slow step at a time. But whilst the other dragons were already sweating and guarding their eyes Yoshiko discovered he was finding it easy. He moved quickly into the outer pit, and up to the line which divided it from the centre. He then waited a few moments to watch the other younglings approach; Igorr was the first to draw up alongside him.

"Enjoying the heat Yoshiko?" he said. "You won't last two minutes in here. I can see you sweating already."

A kind of calm stole over Yoshiko "It's hardly hot at all" he replied. And on a sudden whim he stepped forward over the line, and into the deeper part of the pit.

A gasp went up from the crowd. No youngling had ever ventured beyond into such reaches. There was a roar from the sidelines. "Go on Igorr!" It was Gandar, shouting at his son. "Don't let the Nephan beat you!" he yelled. "Go after him!"

Igorr's face was frightened, but he took a step deeper into the pit. His thin snout twisted in pain.

"Hurry Igorr!" shouted Gandar. "You've been training all year to win this!"

Yoshiko was aware that Igorr was behind him, but he walked onwards towards the very hottest part.

He heard a hiss and turned to see Igorr had fallen back. But to Yoshiko only now was the heat nearly as strong as inside the volcano. He sat carefully in the very centre of the Fire Pit, and in his mind he saw the sorrel juice, grinding the herbs and pouring water into the cauldron. He felt good.

Another call went up and Yoshiko opened his eyes to see that the crowd were on their feet applauding, and the Fire Pit event was over for the younglings. Slowly he walked back out of the pit, allowing the heat to fall from his scales.

The noise of his audience was deafening as he

stepped forward, and it was Ayo who greeted him first.

"No youngling has ever been able to endure that heat," he announced. "And Yoshiko has gone further even than the older dragons. So for this game he has earned the highest honour – The Fire Spear!"

The assembled dragons erupted in applause and Yoshiko took the spear in a daze. He held it aloft to see Ketu and Kiara smiling and waving in the crowd.

Ayo patted him. "Time to say some words," he said. "The stage is yours."

"Fellow dragons!" said Yoshiko. "It is my proudest moment to hold this spear, and I am even prouder to hold it at a time of harmony for Dragor!" The words seemed to be tumbling forth as the dragons made more cheer. "We are all made in rock and stone as well as air and fire. And though we lost something when we left the land of man, it has been returned to us!" He pointed at the charms in their dazzling colours, which hung around the necks of the various clans. "Still we have not learned everything," he concluded. "We must continue to work to recognise our individual talents. The future is ours to be decided."

Ketu and Kiara looked amazed to see their little hatchling now grown into a young warrior making a speech in total confidence to all of Dragor, and Cindina, Amlie and Elsy looked on in admiration at their friend.

"May we live as dragons in harmony forever more," he continued. "All of Dragor will prosper."

As he stepped down clutching the spear and taking in the delighted faces of his elders, Yoshiko knew he had finally achieved Guya's mission for him.

The End

In more Dragor adventures...

A red Guard Dragon made his way purposefully through the assembled clans. The Guard stopped next to Kinga, gave a short bow and then whispered something in his ear. Yoshiko turned to see that the head of the clans had lost the colour in his face.

Now it was the turn of the audience to become anxious. What had disturbed their leader?

"Dragons of Dragor!" announced Kinga. "It is my great misfortune to bring terrible news. This New Birth's Eve we have enjoyed the traditional Fire Games whilst our dragons expecting hatchlings have been guarding their eggs."

"But this guard tells me that an egg has gone missing!"

A great gasp went up from the crowd. Never in their history had such a thing happened.

"From which clan?" one dragon shouted.

"It is from the Saiga clan," said Kinga. "But it does not matter what colour of dragon has had this misfortune befall them. We must all come together."

Yoshiko felt a dark feeling grow in the pit of his stomach. He had been outside Dragor and taken with him a map. Could a human have somehow followed him back here and stolen an egg? It was unthinkable to imagine another dragon could be responsible. He lowered the spear slowly remembering the rainbow and

276

how it had seemed to him a sign of hope and joy.

Yoshiko had thought he was helping the clans in bringing the healing stones. But had he actually brought a terrible harm to Dragor..?

Look out for future books in The Land of Dragor series

Visit the magical & mystical Land of Dragor!

www.landofdragor.com

Web design by Creare Communications Ltd

www.crearedesign.co.uk

Enter the cave of jewels & cauldrons where the wise Guya will help you discover your destiny and secrets untold.

Dragor … where dragons, myths, fairytales and legends are reality!